*The Great Brain
at the Academy*

The Great Brain at the Academy

by *John D. Fitzgerald*

ILLUSTRATED BY MERCER MAYER

A YEARLING BOOK

Published by
DELL PUBLISHING CO., INC.
1 Dag Hammarskjold Plaza
New York, New York 10017

ISBN: 0-440-43113-1

Reprinted by arrangement with The Dial Press

Printed in the United States of America
Seventh Dell Printing—January 1978

For Rt. Rev. Msgr. A. F. Giovannoni

Contents

The Great Brain
at the Academy

CHAPTER ONE

Tom Spots a Card Shark

WHEN MY BROTHER TOM began telling people in Adenville, Utah, that he had a great brain everybody laughed at him, including his own family. We all thought he was trying to play some kind of a kid's joke on us. But after he had used his great brain to swindle all the kids in town and make fools of a lot of grownups nobody laughed at my brother anymore.

I think that was why just about everybody in town except his own family was glad to see Tom leave Adenville on September 1, 1897. And I couldn't help thinking that Papa must have felt kind of relieved too, although he didn't show it. Papa was editor and publisher of the *Aden-*

3

ville Weekly Advocate and was considered one of the smartest men in town. But some of the shenanigans Tom had pulled with his great brain were enough to make Papa feel like a blooming idiot. Now he wouldn't have to worry about men dropping into his office to complain that Tom had swindled their sons. Mamma cried a lot at the depot but she also must have felt at least a little relief. She wouldn't have to worry for the next nine months about mothers telephoning her to complain about Tom. The truth of the matter, though, was that although Tom had been a junior-grade confidence man since he was eight years old, he had never really cheated anybody. With his great brain he simply devised schemes that made people swindle themselves.

Tom and my eldest brother Sweyn were bound for the Catholic Academy for Boys in Salt Lake City. We only had a one-room schoolhouse in Adenville, where Mr. Standish taught the first through the sixth grades. Any parents wanting their kids to get a higher education had to send them to Salt Lake City. Tom was only eleven going on twelve but so smart that Mr. Standish had let him skip the fifth grade. Sweyn was two years older and going back to the academy for his second year. A stranger who saw us three brothers together would never have guessed we were related. Sweyn looked like our Danish-American mother, with blond hair and a light complexion. I had dark unruly hair and dark eyes, just like Papa. Tom didn't look like either Mamma or Papa unless you sort of put them together, and he was the only one in the family who had freckles.

Tom promised to write to me every week. The first letter I received told me how he had spotted a card shark

4

on the train. I didn't find out all the details, though, until my brothers came home for Christmas vacation. Then I got Sweyn to tell me what had happened and later Tom told me what had happened. But there was something wrong. Sweyn didn't mention several things Tom told me. And Tom didn't mention his invention for trains which Sweyn told me all about. That is why I figure the only way to tell what really happened is to put their stories together and tell it in my own way.

Tom admitted he felt down in the dumps as the train pulled out of Adenville. I couldn't blame him. It was the first time he had ever been away from home. I knew when I became old enough to go to the academy that I would probably bawl like a baby.

"Go ahead and cry," Sweyn said as the train left the depot. "It is nothing to be ashamed about. I know I did last year my first time away from home."

Tom sure wanted to cry but he wasn't going to give Sweyn the satisfaction of knowing it. "Maybe I don't feel like crying," he lied.

"Pardon me," Sweyn said sarcastically. "I just thought being separated from Mom and Dad and our kid brother for the first time might make you feel sad. Well, I know something that will make you cry. You won't be able to swindle the kids at the academy and get away with shenanigans like you pulled in Adenville. Those Jesuit priests are strict."

Sweyn's superior big-brother attitude was beginning to get on Tom's nerves. "You are just jealous of my great brain," he said. "It is warm in here. I'm going to open a window."

"You do and you'll get a cinder in your eye," Sweyn said.

That was enough to make Tom open the window even if he got ten cinders in his eyes. He had never let Sweyn boss him around at home and he wasn't about to start now. Sure enough, he got a cinder in his eye. He pulled his head inside quickly and shut the window.

"What did I tell you?" Sweyn said.

"Take the corner of your handkerchief and get it out," Tom said.

"Say please," Sweyn said, smiling and pretending he enjoyed seeing Tom suffer.

"Never mind," Tom said. "I'll go to the washroom and get it out myself."

"I was just joking," Sweyn said, taking out his handkerchief.

He got the cinder out of Tom's eye just as the conductor came into the coach. The conductor was a big ruddy-faced man wearing the traditional blue uniform and cap with a big gold watch chain across his vest. When he came to them he took their tickets and placed two blue stubs under the metal tabs on the seats. Then he looked at Tom's red eye.

"I see it didn't take you long to learn not to open a window on a train, sonny," he said.

Being called "sonny" always made Tom angry. "My name is Tom Fitzgerald, not sonny," he said. "And I can't help wondering why they don't put screens on coach windows so passengers won't get cinders in their eyes."

"Well now, Tom Fitzgerald," the conductor said, "it just so happens that on the newer coaches on the main line we do have screens on the windows. But you still can't open a window when the train is moving."

"Why not?" Tom asked.

"Smoke from the locomotive would get into the passenger cars," the conductor said.

"They could fix it so all windows could be opened without any cinders or smoke getting into the passenger cars," Tom said, although he didn't have the least idea of exactly how it could be done.

"And just how would they do that?" the conductor asked. "I'm sure the president of this railroad and of every other railroad would be delighted to know."

Tom didn't miss seeing the conductor wink at the other passengers. He tapped his index finger to his temple. "I'll put my great brain to work on it," he said, "and let you know when you finish collecting tickets."

"I'll be back," the conductor said. "I wouldn't miss hearing this for the world."

All the passengers in the coach except Sweyn began to laugh. Sweyn felt so embarrassed that he slid way down in his seat. "You have only been on this train for about ten minutes," he said, "and you've already made us the laughing stock of everybody in this coach."

"They won't be laughing very long," Tom said, confident that his great brain would not let him down.

"You must be plumb loco," Sweyn said with disgust. "They have engineers with years of experience designing trains. If there was any way to open windows without getting cinders and smoke into the passenger cars they would have invented it."

Do you think that made Tom give up? Heck no.

"The men who built Conestoga wagons and prairie schooners never thought of putting brakes on them," he said. "Thousands of emigrants who came West had to chain their rear wheels when going down a grade. Then one day one of them got tired of chaining his wheels. He used a shovel handle, a couple of two-by-fours to make a lever, a wooden block, a piece of rope, and the sole of one of his old shoes and made a brake for his wagon. Now please be quiet while I put my great brain to work."

Tom's great brain must have been working like sixty because when the conductor returned he was ready.

"Here I am, Tom Fitzgerald," the conductor said with a smile on his ruddy face. "Now tell me how we can open windows on trains without getting cinders or smoke in the cars."

Tom wasn't about to divulge his plan for nothing. When he put his great brain to work he expected to be paid for it.

"I'll expect some financial reward if the railroad uses my idea," he said.

"Naturally," the conductor said. "And you have all these passengers as witnesses that it was your idea."

"They could run a pipe from the smokestack on the locomotive along the top of the train to the caboose," Tom said, "and let all the cinders and smoke out behind the train."

"I'm afraid that wouldn't work," the conductor said. "The pipe would break when the train went around a curve."

"Not if they put flexible couplings on it between each car," Tom said.

8

A salesman across the aisle began to laugh. "I think the boy has you there, conductor," he said.

"No he hasn't," the conductor said. "With such a long pipe the fire under the boiler in the locomotive would go out."

This stumped Tom until he remembered a photograph of a factory he had seen in a magazine. "I don't think it would," he said, "because the longer the smokestack the better it draws. That is why they put such high chimneys on factories."

By this time Tom was so sure his idea would work that he began to wonder how big a reward the railroad would give him. The conductor must have guessed what he was thinking.

"I'm afraid you will never collect that reward," he said. "In order for a smokestack to work it has to be vertical. Hot air is lighter than cold air. What creates a draft is the hot air rising to the top. If you bent the smokestack over horizontally the hot air would just rise to the bend in the pipe and be trapped there. And as a result you would have no draft and the fire in the firebox of the locomotive would go out."

No wonder Tom didn't mention anything about this in his letter to me. And no wonder Sweyn chuckled when he told me about it at Christmastime. It wasn't until I confronted Tom with what Sweyn had said that I learned the whole story. And it just goes to prove a fellow has to listen to both sides of a story to learn the truth.

Tom admitted he was stunned that there was a flaw in his idea that he felt as if the conductor had hit him on the head with a baseball bat. And even worse was the

shock to his money-loving heart. And boy, oh, boy, was he embarrassed as the conductor and all the passengers except Sweyn began laughing at him. Papa had often said that when a fellow starts out trying to make a fool of somebody else he usually ends up making a fool of himself. And that is exactly what happened to Tom. But there was one thing Papa and Mamma had drilled into us boys and that was always to face up to our problems.

"I deserve to be laughed at," Tom said to the conductor. "I tried to make a fool out of you and ended up being the fool."

"Don't take it so hard, Tom," the conductor said sympathetically. "Some of our greatest inventors were laughed at. You just keep on using that great brain of yours and someday you *will* invent something that will improve trains."

"In that case," he said, "I've got to learn all about trains by the time we get to Salt Lake City. Can I come with you?"

"Come along," the conductor said, smiling.

When they got to the caboose the conductor introduced himself as Harold Walters and the brakeman as Paul Jackson.

"Why do you ride in the caboose instead of in the coach?" Tom asked.

"This is what we call a feeder line," Mr. Walters said. "On feeder lines we don't have a train that is strictly for passengers like we do on the main line. This train, for example, has a mail-and-baggage car, a freight car, and sometimes a car for livestock in addition to a smoking car and a coach car. And because the train is what you could call

11

part of a freight train we have a caboose like they do on all freight trains. On the main-line passenger trains the conductor and brakeman have a seat reserved for them on one of the coaches."

Tom remained with Mr. Walters for almost three hours, going with the conductor to the coach and smoking cars to collect tickets at each stop. Then he returned to his seat.

"Well," Sweyn said, "did my little brother learn all about choo-choo trains?"

Tom figured this was as good a time as any to put an end to this big-brother act of Sweyn's. And he knew the hardest blow of all would be in the pocketbook.

"I guess you know a lot more about trains than I do," he said.

"Why shouldn't I?" Sweyn asked in that superior way of older brothers. "I have already made two trips to Salt Lake City and back."

"You sure have," Tom said, "and I figure for every mile I've ridden on a train you must have traveled at least twenty. Right?"

"Right," Sweyn said.

"That means you know twenty times more about trains than I do," Tom said. "Right?"

"Yeah," Sweyn answered.

"Then put your money where your mouth is," Tom said. "I'll bet you a quarter that I can ask you two questions about trains that you can't answer. If you answer both of them you win. If you only answer one of them it is a tie and the bet is off."

"Get your quarter ready," Sweyn said confidently,

"and go ahead and ask your two questions."

"Who is the big boss on a train, the conductor or the engineer?" Tom asked.

"That is easy," Sweyn said. "The engineer is."

"One wrong," Tom said. "And you can ask Mr. Walters the conductor if you don't believe me. Now for the second question. What were conductors on trains called before they were called conductors?"

"What kind of a question is that?" Sweyn asked.

"It is about trains, isn't it?" Tom asked, smiling. "I can see you don't know the answer so I will tell you. They were called captains because they had full command of a train just like the captain of a ship. Now fork over that quarter."

Poor old Sweyn was as foolish for making that bet as a rooster trying to lay an egg. I don't remember my eldest brother or me ever winning a bet from Tom. Sweyn handed Tom twenty-five cents.

When the train arrived in Cedar City a man wearing a white cap and jacket boarded the train and went into the smoking car. As the train left the depot he came into the coach. In front of him he had a box-type tray held by a strap around his neck.

"Candy, peanuts, chewing gum, and magazines!" he called out.

Tom stared at the man as a passenger bought a candy bar and a magazine. "Who is that?" he asked.

"The candy butcher," Sweyn answered. "And it just goes to prove you don't know everything about trains."

"Why do they call him a butcher?" Tom asked. "Butchers only work in meat markets."

13

"How should I know?" Sweyn said.

"Which just goes to prove you don't know everything about trains," Tom said.

"One thing I do know," Sweyn said. "If you want any candy you had better buy it now and eat it before we get to Salt Lake City. The superintendent, Father Rodriguez, only allows each student to buy ten cents worth of candy once every four weeks. And parents are forbidden to mail any sweets to their sons or bring any candy on visiting days."

The academy was beginning to sound like a reform school to Tom. "What has he got against candy?" he asked.

"He says it is bad for the teeth and health," Sweyn answered. "And if you have any candy when you get there he will take it away from you."

"Don't worry about it," Tom said. "My great brain will figure out a way for us to have all the candy we want."

"You get caught smuggling candy into the academy and you'll get demerits and punishment," Sweyn said. "And if you get twenty demerits in one month you can be expelled."

"What kind of punishment?" Tom asked.

"Peeling potatoes in the kitchen, cleaning the washrooms, mopping and waxing the floors, and things like that," Sweyn answered.

"They've got to catch you first," Tom said confidently. "I'm getting hungry. Let's eat."

They got down from the rack the shoe box containing the lunch Mamma had made for them. When Mamma prepared a lunch she always made sure nobody went hungry. There was enough for six people. Tom and Sweyn ate their fill. There were still five pieces of fried chicken, four hard-boiled eggs, five bread-and-butter sandwiches, and three pieces of chocolate cake left.

The traveling salesman across the aisle spoke to Tom. "The train doesn't stop for passengers to eat until we get to Provo," he said. "I'll give you a dime for one of those drumsticks and a bread-and-butter sandwich."

"How about a hard-boiled egg and a piece of cake too?" Tom asked. The smell of money to him was just like the smell of food to a hungry man. "It will only cost you another dime."

"Sold," the salesman said.

Sweyn was shaking his head as Tom pocketed the twenty cents. "You can't even ride on a train without turning conniver," he said. "Mom would have a fit if she knew what you just did."

"The customer is perfectly satisfied," Tom said. "And that gives me an idea. There must be other hungry passengers on this train. I'm going to sell the rest of this stuff."

"You can't do that," Sweyn protested. "Only the candy butcher can sell things on a train."

Did this make Tom give up his idea? Heck no. When it came to money he was like a bloodhound on the trail of a fugitive.

"Then I'll make a deal with the candy butcher," he said.

Tom found the candy butcher sitting on the rear seat in the smoking car. "Let me sell this food on the train," he said, "and I'll buy candy with all the money I get. Is it a deal?"

"It sure is," the candy butcher said. "See those four

men playing poker on a suitcase at the other end of the car? They were complaining because I don't sell sandwiches like they do on the main line. Try them.''

Tom walked to the other end of the smoking car. "The candy butcher told me you men were hungry," he said. "A piece of home-fried chicken and a bread-and-butter sandwich will cost you a dime. The hard-boiled eggs are a nickel and the cake ten cents.''

Tom collected seventy-five cents from the hungry poker players and then stood watching the game. The men were playing stud poker. A man the other players called Mr. Harrison was winning and a man named Baylor who looked like a rancher was the big loser. The other two players were complaining about losing also. Tom watched while four hands were played and he knew why Mr. Harrison was winning. He decided to tell Mr. Walters about it. He stopped and gave the candy butcher the seventy-five cents, saying he would get the candy later. He found Mr. Walters in the caboose with the brakeman.

"Is it part of your job to watch out for card sharks?" he asked.

"It certainly is, Tom," the conductor said. "You see, whenever a passenger loses money to a card shark on a train he never blames the card shark or himself. He always blames the railroad. Why do you ask?''

"Those four men playing poker in the smoking car are using a marked deck of cards," Tom answered.

Mr. Walters looked as surprised as a man who opens a can of beans and finds peas inside instead. "You must be mistaken," he said. "I inspected that deck of cards before the men started to play, and my years of experience as a conductor have taught me just about every way a deck can be marked."

"These cards are marked at the factory," Tom said. "My uncle, Mark Trainor, is the marshal and deputy sheriff in Adenville and he showed me a deck just like it. A salesman selling playing cards came to town. He offered both saloonkeepers such a good price that they each bought fifty decks of cards. A week later a man calling himself Harry Johnson came to town and began playing poker in both saloons. He won so much money that the players said he was either the luckiest poker player in the world or a card cheat. But nobody could prove he was cheating and he kept on winning money every night. Uncle Mark knew nobody could be that lucky. He got a deck of the cards from a saloonkeeper and took it to his office. He studied it for hours before he discovered how they were marked at the factory. He arrested Harry Johnson, who confessed he and the card salesman were partners."

Mr. Walters nodded his head. "That was a slick confidence game," he said. "The salesman got the cards into the saloons and then his partner came along and, using the marked cards, had to win. I didn't like the looks of that Harrison fellow with his manicured nails and waxed moustache. They are his cards."

They went to the smoking car and waited until the poker players finished playing a hand. Mr. Harrison won again. Then Mr. Walters picked up the deck of cards.

"What is the idea?" Mr. Harrison asked. "You checked these cards and so did these three gentlemen before we started to play."

"Then you won't mind if my friend here takes a look

17

at them," Mr. Walters said, handing the deck to Tom.

"That's the kid who sold us the food," Mr. Harrison said. "What is this, some kind of a joke?"

The moment Tom spotted the marked deck of cards he had put his great brain to work on how to take financial advantage of the situation. He looked at Mr. Walters.

"If I can prove this deck is marked, will Mr. Harrison have to return all the money he has won?" he said.

"He certainly will," the conductor said.

Then Tom looked at the three losing poker players. "I figure it should be worth a dollar apiece to you to know how these cards are marked so you can get your money back," he said.

Mr. Baylor nodded his head. "You figure right, boy," he said.

Tom held the deck with the faces down and dealt out five piles of cards with just four cards in four of the piles and the rest in the fifth pile.

"This deck has a small diamond design on the back like most playing cards," Tom said. "The diamonds are arranged at the place where the cards are manufactured, so anybody who knows the secret can tell how many high cards the other players have by looking at the backs."

He pointed at one of the piles. "These four cards have full diamonds across the top and bottom edges, which means they are the four aces," he said.

Mr. Baylor turned the four cards over, revealing the four aces.

Tom pointed at another pile. "These four cards have half diamonds across the top and bottom edges, which means they are the four kings," he said.

18

Mr. Baylor turned over the four kings.

"And this pile," Tom said, "has quarter diamonds across the top and bottom edges, which means they are the four queens."

Mr. Baylor turned over the four queens.

"This last pile of four cards," Tom said, "has full diamonds down both sides, which means they are the four jacks." He turned over the four jacks himself. "All the other cards in the deck have staggered full and half diamonds on all four edges. Mr. Harrison could tell by looking at the backs of your cards whether you had an ace, king, queen, or jack as a hole card playing stud poker, and playing draw poker he could tell how many high cards you held in your hands."

Mr. Baylor slammed his fist down on the suitcase. "You low-down skunk of a card cheat," he said to Mr. Harrison. "I'm going to drag you off this train at the next stop and beat you to a pulp."

"Simmer down," Mr. Walters said. "As soon as Mr. Harrison returns all the money he has won from you gentlemen I will take him to the caboose and handcuff him to a seat. He and the deck of cards will be turned over to the police when we get to Salt Lake City. It will then be up to you men to go to police headquarters and sign a complaint."

And that is how Tom spotted a card shark and made himself three dollars richer on his first train trip. Papa had once said that if Tom fell down into a deep hole, instead of breaking a leg The Great Brain would probably discover a gold mine. But the way Tom ended his first letter almost made a nervous wreck out of me waiting for his next to arrive. And here is why.

"This has been a long letter, J.D.," Tom wrote. "So I will have to wait until my next letter to tell you about the rest of my first train ride and the most exciting experience of my life. When you tell the kids in Adenville about it they will all turn green with envy."

CHAPTER TWO

Tom at the Throttle

ALL WEEK I WONDERED what could possibly
have happened to Tom on his first train ride that made it
the most exciting experience of his life. When I finally received his second letter I understood why he had said that
all the kids in town would turn green with envy. When I
showed the kids the letter they didn't actually turn green
any more than a yellow-bellied coward has a yellow belly.
But you never saw such a bunch of envious kids in your
life.

When Tom came home for the Christmas vacation
with Sweyn he told Papa, Mamma, Aunt Bertha, our four-
year-old foster brother Frankie, and me all about riding in

21

the locomotive from Provo to Salt Lake City. Hearing him tell it was ten times more exciting than reading about it. Tom's great brain had already figured this out. He charged the kids two cents apiece to enter our barn and listen to him personally tell about his exciting experience. And every kid in town from four years old to sixteen was there.

I, of course, had to get Sweyn's side of the story, which was a little different from Tom's story. But by putting both together I can tell just about exactly what did happen:

After collecting his three dollars from the grateful poker players Tom went to the other end of the smoking car and sat down beside the candy butcher. He collected the seventy-five-cents worth of candy that the man owed him.

"Why do they call you a butcher?" he asked.

"It is a show business slang word," the candy butcher said. "In vaudeville and burlesque theaters men who sell candy during intermission are called candy butchers. When men began selling candy and things on trains the name just stuck."

"I don't see how you make any money," Tom said. "The train fare must eat up all the profits."

"I ride the trains free," the candy butcher said. "My run is from Cedar City to Ogden and back."

Tom returned to his seat and dumped fifteen five-cent bars of candy on it. "I made a deal with the candy butcher," he told Sweyn. "He let me sell the rest of our lunch if I'd buy candy with it. I got seventy-five cents."

"Half of that lunch was mine," Sweyn said. "You got twenty cents from the salesman and seventy-five cents more, which makes ninety-five cents. You can have the odd nickel because you did all the work. Just give me my forty-five cents in cash."

Poor old Sweyn was a dreamer if he thought he was going to talk The Great Brain out of forty-five cents.

"If I remember correctly," Tom said, "you told me I was a conniver for selling part of the lunch and Mamma would have a fit if she knew about it. I sure as heck don't want it on my conscience that I made a conniver out of my own brother and made him partly responsible for our mother having a fit. So I will just keep all the profits and my conscience will be clear. But dividing the profits and giving my brother some candy are two different things. Help yourself to as many bars as you can eat."

Sweyn knew when he was beat. He helped himself to a chocolate bar and a peanut bar. Tom put one bar of candy in his pocket. Then he got down his suitcase and put the remaining twelve bars of candy between his clothing.

Sweyn stared at him bug-eyed. "Just what do you think you are doing?" he asked.

"If the fellows at the academy are only allowed ten cents worth of candy every four weeks," Tom said, "I shouldn't have any trouble selling these five-cent bars of candy for a dime each. And once I get my candy store going I'll make a fortune."

"Have you gone plumb loco?" Sweyn asked. "What candy store?"

Tom closed his suitcase and put it back on the rack. "The candy store I'm going to open at the academy," he said, rubbing his hands together. "I'll double my money on every bar of candy I sell."

"No you won't," Sweyn said. "There is no possible

way for you to smuggle enough candy into the academy to start a candy store. And I'm not going to let you smuggle in even those twelve bars. I'll tell Father Rodriguez they are in your suitcase."

Tom was as flabbergasted as a duck who discovers it can't swim. "Do you mean to tell me you would inform on your own brother?" he asked.

"I can't help it," Sweyn said. "I promised Mom and Dad that I would keep an eye on you. And if you get into any trouble they are going to blame me."

Tom munched on his bar of candy while he put his great brain to work. "I sure feel sorry for you if you do tell," he finally said. "That would force me to tell all the kids at the academy that my big brother is a tattletale. And that, S.D., will make you about as popular as a skunk in a parlor."

Sweyn was beat and knew it. "That's blackmail," he said. "But all right. I want a signed statement from you that any trouble you get into at the academy is your own fault. I'll need it to show to Mom and Dad when you get expelled."

"That is fair enough," Tom said.

He got down his suitcase and removed a notebook and pencil from it. Holding the suitcase on his knees he wrote:

To Whom It May Concern:

No matter what happens to me at the Catholic Academy for Boys I take all the blame personally.

T. D. Fitzgerald

He tore the page from the notebook and handed it to Sweyn. "Does that satisfy you?" he asked.

Sweyn read the note. "I'm satisfied," he said.

Tom was no dummy. He handed the pencil and notebook to Sweyn. "Now write what I tell you," he said. *"To whom it may concern: I promise not to interfere with anything my brother does at the Catholic Academy for Boys.* And sign it."

Sweyn wrote the statement and handed it to Tom. "I'm not interfering," he said. "Just giving you some brotherly advice. Every once in a while they have an inspection at the academy. The priests search your locker, desk, suitcase, and any other place you might hide candy or magazines we aren't supposed to read or anything else that might be forbidden."

"That is my worry now, not yours," Tom said. Then he took the three silver dollars from his pocket and began jingling them in his hand.

"Where did you get all that money?" Sweyn asked, as astonished as could be.

Tom told him about the marked deck of cards and the poker players. Sweyn couldn't help feeling a little envious. Tom had made a neat profit of four dollars and twenty cents on his first train ride and twenty-five cents of that was formerly Sweyn's money. Papa had often said when a person starts to envy another person the devil is right there to whisper in his ear. Right then the devil was whispering to Sweyn how he could get even.

"The money won't do you any good at the academy," he said. "There is no place to spend it."

"What's the matter with spending it outside the academy?" Tom asked.

"We only get outside the walls one day every four weeks," Sweyn said. "Father Rodriguez or one of the other priests is always with us even then. And all you can spend is ten cents for candy."

"If you can't spend any money, where do you go?" Tom asked.

"Sometimes the priests take us on a nature-study hike or a picnic," Sweyn said. "Sometimes we just go sight-seeing or to the museum or art gallery. And once in a while as a treat we get to go to the Salt Lake Theater. Buying a ticket to get in is the only way you can spend any money."

"What about sports?" Tom asked.

Sweyn was really enjoying the look of dismay on Tom's face. "What sports?" he asked. "The only athletics at the academy is one hour of calisthenics in the gymnasium on school days. And the gym is nothing but an old barn with a hardwood floor."

By this time Tom was almost wishing he had been born a Mormon or a Protestant. "You never told Papa and Mamma it was like a prison," he said.

"I'm no crybaby," Sweyn said. And then he really poured salt in Tom's wounds. "Thank the Lord this is my last year at the academy, because they only have the seventh and eighth grades. Next year I'll be going to high school in Pennsylvania and living with some of Papa's relatives. And while I'm enjoying myself there I promise I'll think of you often, little brother, and of how you are suffering at the academy."

Tom felt so down in the dumps he didn't even get angry at the "little brother" bit. Sweyn made the academy sound as if all the students had to wear striped suits with numbers on them. He knew there was only one thing to do.

"No candy, no sports, no nothing," he said. "I guess I'll have to put my great brain to work on it and get some changes made at the academy."

"The only thing you will change will be yourself," Sweyn said, "from an enrolled student to an expelled student. The Jesuit priests are plenty sharp because they have been dealing with boys for years. You won't be able to put anything over on them."

Did that discourage Tom? Heck no. He was confident he could make life easier for himself and the other kids at the academy.

A few minutes later Mr. Walters came into the coach. "Provo is the next stop," he called out. "There will be a twenty-minute stopover for passengers to get something to eat. The dining room is located right next to the depot."

Sweyn stood up when the train stopped. "I'm going to get a glass of milk and piece of pie in the dining room," he said.

"Go ahead," Tom said. "I'm not hungry."

Tom wasn't just twisting a lamb's tail trying to make it bark like a dog when he said he had to learn all about trains by the time he arrived in Salt Lake City. But how could he if he didn't get to ride in the locomotive? He realized it was something every kid dreams about but only one in a million ever gets to do.

He got off the train with Sweyn and walked up to where the locomotive was preparing to take on water and coal. He had seen many locomotives in Adenville but this was the first time it had entered his mind that they were things of beauty. The locomotive had the number *205* on the round brass plate on its nose, a shiny brass bell, a whistle and headlight, a blue steel belly, and gigantic wheels. With smoke coming from the smokestack and steam escaping from the cylinders it was almost as if the locomotive was a living thing.

Tom walked back and waited for Mr. Walters to come out of the stationmaster's office.

"Think they will ever have it so passengers can eat right on a train?" he asked.

"It is coming, Tom," the conductor said. "We already have sleeping cars on the main line invented by a man named Pullman. And a man named Fred Harvey is working on a dining car that will serve hot meals right on the train."

"You sure have taught me a lot about trains," Tom said. "But I'll never know all I should unless you fix it so I can ride in the locomotive from here to Salt Lake City."

"I can't do that, Tom," Mr. Walters said. "It is against regulations."

The conductor didn't know it but he had walked right into Tom's trap.

"It is also against regulations to let card sharks operate on trains," Tom said. "This Harrison fellow could have gone on cheating passengers for years if it hadn't been for me. And you can report how these crooked decks of cards are marked at the factory so other conductors will know how to spot them. I figure the railroad owes me something for that."

Mr. Walters nodded. "When you put it that way," he said, "I agree the railroad owes you a ride in the locomotive. But you'll get your clothes all dirty."

Tom was so happy he wanted to do a little dance. "I've got a rain slicker and rain hat in my suitcase I can wear."

28

"Go get them," Mr. Walters said. "But come up to the locomotive on the other side of the train. I don't want the stationmaster to see you. I haven't time to explain to him right now."

Sweyn was back in his seat when Tom entered the coach. He stared bug-eyed as Tom opened the suitcase and put on his rain slicker and hat.

"Have you gone plumb loco?" he asked. "It isn't raining. And even if it was you can't get wet in here."

"I'm going to ride in the locomotive and don't want to get my clothes dirty," Tom said.

"In a pig's eye," Sweyn said.

"Just make sure you take my suitcase off the train when we get to Salt Lake City," Tom said.

Poor Sweyn just sat there with his mouth open as he watched Tom leave the coach.

Tom ran around to the other side of the train and up to the locomotive. He could hear Mr. Walters talking to the engineer.

"Got a passenger for you, Ed, from here to Salt Lake City," the conductor said. "He is a boy about eleven or twelve years old. He has a curious mind and will ask you a lot of questions."

"I get it," Ed said. "He must be the son of some big shot on the railroad."

"I haven't time to explain now," Mr. Walters said. "Just make sure he gets off on the opposite side from the depot so the stationmaster doesn't see him. You'll find him waiting on the other side now."

A moment later the engineer put his head out of the cab window. "Come on up to the deck, boy," he said.

Tom was so excited he almost slipped and fell as he

climbed into the cab of the locomotive. The engineer was wearing blue overalls, a blue shirt, and a blue cap with a long visor. He had a red bandanna handkerchief tied around his neck. The fireman was dressed the same but his face, hands, and clothing were covered with coal dust.

"My name is Ed," the engineer said, "and the fireman's name is Bill. What is your name, boy?"

"Tom Fitzgerald," Tom answered.

The engineer scratched his forehead. "Funny," he said, "but I never heard of any big shot on this railroad by that name."

Tom knew he'd better change the subject quickly. "Why did you tell me to come up to the deck?" he asked. "I thought only boats had decks."

"The platform of a locomotive is called the deck by railroad men," Ed answered. "Now stand back from the gangway so Bill can slug the firebox."

Tom stepped back. He watched the fireman use the end of a scoop shovel to open the door of the firebox. He was surprised at the intense heat coming from the burning coal. He watched Bill stoke the firebox with coal taken from the tender.

"That ought to take care of it until we get to Salt Lake City," Bill said, shutting the door of the firebox.

"We are going to have to pound her to make up for the few minutes we are late," Ed said.

Tom was puzzled. "I understood 'gangway' meant the rear part of the deck," he said. "And I knew when you told Bill to slug the firebox you wanted him to put more coal in it. But what do you mean by 'pounding' her?"

"It is railroad talk meaning we've got to get all the speed we safely can out of this locomotive," Ed said. "See that cord? The one on the left? It rings the bell to let passengers know we will be leaving in a few minutes. Don't yank on it too hard or the bell will just spin around. You can tell by the feel of the cord and the sound of the bell when you are doing it just right."

Boy, oh, boy, was Tom in his glory. He never expected they would let him ring the bell. He had heard locomotive bells many times in Adenville. But the sound of the bell on engine number 205 as he rang it was the most beautiful sound he had ever heard.

"That's enough," Ed said. "I've got to look out the cab window now so I can see when the conductor gives us the highball. 'Highball' is another railroad term, Tom, meaning the arm signal to start. Get your hand on that other cord that blows the whistle. Give it two quick pulls when you hear the conductor call 'All aboard.' "

By this time Tom was more excited than a dog chasing a rabbit. In a couple of minutes he heard Mr. Walters calling, "All aboard!"

Tom jerked the cord twice and heard two short blasts from the steam whistle. "Do we start now?" he asked.

"Not until the conductor gives me the arm signal," Ed said. "There it is. Now grab that handrailing so you don't fall."

Tom took hold of the handrailing. He watched the engineer release the air brakes. Ed turned a valve, then put his left hand on a bar about two feet long with a round handle on one end.

"This used to be called a Johnson bar," Ed said, "but now we call it the throttle. The farther I push it forward the more steam pressure it will release to the cylinders and the faster we will go. I take it nice and easy so we don't jerk the cars we are pulling until we get under way. A steam locomotive is about the simplest machine ever invented. But each one is just a little bit different. You take this one. I have to sort of coax it and drive it by the feel of the throttle."

The train began to move as Ed slowly pushed the throttle forward.

"Why do you say it is a simple machine?" Tom asked.

"It has a firebox into which we put coal to burn," Ed said as the train began to pick up speed. "This heats the water in the boiler, producing steam. The steam is released to each cylinder and its pressure pushes the pistons. The pistons are attached to rods which are connected with the drivers. The steam pressure in the cylinders moves the pistons back and forth, and this moves the rods that make the drivers go around."

"Why do you call the wheels 'drivers'?" Tom asked.

"Because they are the wheels that actually drive the locomotive," Ed answered. "This is an American type 4-4-0 locomotive which means the drive wheels are four-and-a-half feet high. The drivers on a locomotive built to pull a freight train are smaller, which gives the wheels more pulling power. And on fast passenger trains they use locomotives with larger drivers because the bigger the drivers the faster a locomotive can go."

Tom was getting used to the rocking motion of the locomotive and he let go of the handrail. "How fast will number 205 go?" he asked.

"She will do a mile a minute on a straightaway," Ed answered. "And Walters was certainly right. You do have a curious mind."

Tom didn't want the engineer to get bored answering questions. "I'm sorry," he said, "but I must learn all about locomotives by the time we reach Salt Lake City. I won't ask any more questions if you don't want me to though."

"Go ahead and ask all the questions you want," Ed said.

"What is the fastest a train will go?" Tom asked, quickly taking advantage of the offer.

"Engine number 999, pulling the Empire State Express between Syracuse and Buffalo, New York, ran a measured mile at one-hundred-twelve-and-a-half miles per hour back in 1893," Ed said.

"Boy, oh, boy!" Tom exclaimed. "That is really traveling."

"We are coming to a road crossing," Ed said. "Grab the whistle cord and give three long blasts."

Tom pulled the cord. He discovered as long as he held it down the whistle kept on blowing and when he let it up the whistle stopped.

A few minutes later Ed spoke to the fireman. "We are coming to that bad curve now, Bill," he said. "I'm going to take it ten miles above our usual speed. You know what to do."

Tom was astonished as he saw Bill go to the side of the cab opposite the engineer, place his hands against it, and push.

"As long as you are here, Tom," Bill said, "give me a hand so engine number 205 doesn't tip over."

Tom stood beside Bill and began to push. He could hear Bill grunting as if using all his strength as they went around the curve. Tom pushed as hard as he could until he heard both Ed and Bill laughing.

"Don't feel bad about it, Tom," Ed said. "I had a green fireman one time who fell for it too. And to make up for playing a little joke on you, I'm going to let you drive engine 205. No sense in riding in a locomotive if you can't tell your friends you drove one. Get over here in front of me and put your left hand on the throttle and your head out the cab window."

Tom did as he was told.

"We've got a straightaway coming up now for a few miles," Ed said. "I'm going to give it all old number 205 has got."

Tom felt Ed pushing the throttle forward. With his head out the cab window and the wind whistling in his ears, it seemed as if they were flying.

"I'm going to take my hand off the throttle now," the engineer said. "Hold her steady. There you go, Tom. You are now driving number 205 at sixty miles an hour."

Tom said later that was the happiest moment of his life. Many times in his life he had made his great brain work like sixty. But this was the first time he had ever actually traveled at sixty miles an hour. Ed only let him drive the locomotive for about a minute but that was enough.

It was with a feeling of regret that he said good-bye to Ed and Bill when the train arrived at the depot in Salt Lake City.

"Good-bye and thanks," he said. "I'll remember both of you and number 205 for the rest of my life."

"Bill and I enjoyed having you with us," Ed said. "When we were boys your age we both used to dream about riding in a locomotive. I guess that is why we became railroad men."

Tom climbed down the iron rungs of the locomotive to the ground. Then he went around the train to meet Sweyn.

Tom was just about the happiest kid in the world right then. But he sure as heck wasn't a happy kid for long. And if he'd known what lay ahead of him that day he would have probably climbed back into the cab of the locomotive and just kept on going.

CHAPTER THREE

Off on the Wrong Foot

I WAS SURPRISED when Tom wrote me that he had got off on the wrong foot at the academy but that it wasn't anything serious. For my money, any trouble The Great Brain got into had to be serious. Papa was hoping the Jesuit priests would reform Tom. That to me was like hoping the priests would get rid of the freckles on Tom's face. I found out I was right when Father Rodriguez sent the first monthly report on Tom's and Sweyn's progress and deportment. These reports were sent to the parents of all students every month.

Papa always stopped at the post office at the end of his day's work, but he never opened the mail until after supper. Mamma said it was because Papa didn't want to spoil his appetite if there was any bad news in the mail. It was a good system because Papa wouldn't have been able to eat a bite if he'd read the report on Tom before supper.

Papa waited until after the dishes were put away and then read the reports aloud to Mamma, Aunt Bertha, and me in the parlor. He read the report on Sweyn first and when he finished he looked as pleased as a rabbit with two carrots. But by the time he finished Tom's report his cheeks were so blown up with anger I thought he would blow his teeth right out of his mouth.

"I'll wager they expel him and send him home!" he shouted, waving the report in the air like it was a red flag and he was a bull.

Mamma took it very calmly. "He just needs time to adjust," she said.

"Adjust?" Papa cried. "The Great Brain will have a difficult time adjusting in heaven." And then he added, "If he ever gets there."

I didn't blame Papa for being so upset. The report was in polite language but made it very plain that if Tom didn't mend his ways he would be sent home. I didn't get all the details of what had happened until my brothers came home for the Christmas vacation. And, of course, what Tom told me and what Sweyn told me and what Father Rodriguez wrote in his report were three slightly different stories. So I have to be sort of a detective to figure out exactly what happened.

Tom met Sweyn on the platform in back of the depot in Salt Lake City. If there was any truth in that business about people turning green with envy Sweyn would have been the color of our grass in the summertime.

"I thought you were joking," he said, "until the conductor told me you were actually riding in the locomotive. How did you ever pull that off?"

"When a fellow has a great brain, anything is possible," Tom said, taking off the raincoat and hat.

"Well, you had better put your great brain to work on a way to get cleaned up before Father O'Malley sees you," Sweyn said. "You look like a chimney sweep with that soot and coal dust all over your face. Maybe you can sneak into the washroom in the depot and wash up."

But Tom didn't get a chance to wash up. Father O'Malley was waiting for them just inside the doorway of the depot. He was a middle-aged man wearing the traditional black robe and hood of a Jesuit priest. The hood was pushed back on his neck, revealing a head that was bald except for a fringe of hair around the edges. There was a braided cord around his waist and a crucifix hanging from a chain around his neck. His cheeks were rosy red, as if somebody had just pinched them.

"Welcome back, Sweyn," he said as they shook hands. "I trust the good Lord gave you a pleasant journey from Adenville." Then he looked at Tom. "And this must be your brother Thomas, who doesn't look as if he had a pleasant journey at all."

"I rode in the cab of the locomotive from Provo," Tom said proudly, still thrilled by the ride.

"Did you now?" Father O'Malley said. "That is something I've always wanted to do. You must tell me all about it some time, Thomas."

"Please don't call me Thomas," Tom said. "It sounds kind of sissified. Please call me Tom instead."

39

"I doubt if anyone would call your patron saint, Thomas, a sissy," Father O'Malley said. "However, I will call you Tom if you prefer. But Father Rodriguez may take an entirely different point of view."

"Speaking of Father Rodriguez," Sweyn said, "can my brother wash up before we go to the academy?"

"I'm sorry, Sweyn," the priest said. "But my orders are to deliver the out-of-town boys exactly the way they arrive. If it wasn't for this rule they would all want to wash up, clean the dirt from beneath their fingernails, put on a clean shirt and necktie, and anything else that might help make a good first impression on Father Rodriguez."

Sweyn looked at Tom. "That means on your first day you'll get demerits," he said.

Did that bother Tom? Heck no.

"It was worth getting demerits to ride in a locomotive," he said.

He followed Sweyn and the priest out of the depot to where several horse-drawn liveries were waiting. Their drivers were soliciting customers by proclaiming good accommodations and free transportation to the various hotels. Father O'Malley stopped when they came to a single horse hitched to a buggy with two seats. He got into the front seat and Tom and Sweyn climbed into the rear.

"Have you ever been to Salt Lake City before, Tom?" the priest asked.

"No, Father," Tom answered.

"Then I shall give you a very short tour of it," the priest said.

Father O'Malley drove without speaking until they came to Temple Square. "The six-spired gray granite building is the Temple of the Church of Jesus Christ of

Latter-day Saints," he said. "Construction was begun in 1853 but it wasn't completed until forty years later. The big building with a roof that resembles the back of a huge tortoise is the Mormon Tabernacle. The acoustics are remarkable. You can drop a pin at one end and hear it drop at the other end two hundred feet away."

Tom had read all about the temple and tabernacle. But what excited him most were the horse-drawn streetcars, the tall buildings, and the crowds of people as they drove down Main Street.

They left the business district and Father O'Malley pointed out Saint Mary's Academy for Catholic Girls and the Presbyterian Westminster College. After seeing these two schools Tom was very disappointed when they arrived at the Catholic Academy. Sweyn had told him it had once been the home of a wealthy Catholic who had donated it to the Jesuits for a school. Tom didn't blame the wealthy Catholic for not wanting to live there anymore. It might have been a nice neighborhood at one time but now the big homes had been turned into cheap rooming houses or torn down to make way for factories and warehouses.

The academy itself was a three-story wooden building with dormer windows in the attic, making it look four stories tall. Its white paint was a dirty gray color from the smokestacks of surrounding factories and so blistered with age that it was peeling from some of the boards. One side of the academy was flush up against the sidewalk. The other three sides were enclosed within a high rock wall that had a gate at the front entrance.

Tom had to admit the grounds looked nice with trees and shrubs and a green lawn. But one thing surprised him. There were statues of saints all over the place. It

41

looked as if every Catholic in Salt Lake City had donated a statue of his patron saint. A gravel circular driveway led up to the entrance, where there was a huge statue of Saint Ignatius Loyola, founder of the Society of Jesus.

"Well, Tom," Father O'Malley said as they stopped at the entrance. "What do you think of the academy?"

"Well, if you don't mind my saying so, Father," Tom said, "I think it could use a little more paint and a few less statues."

"You are so right," the priest agreed. "But I suppose we should thank the Lord that enough money was donated to remodel the home into an academy. You boys go right in. Father Rodriguez is expecting you. I must return this horse and buggy to the livery stable."

Tom followed Sweyn up stone steps and into the academy. They entered a long hallway with white painted walls and a highly polished hardwood floor. There was a statue of Saint Paul in one corner, one of Saint Anthony in another corner, and between them a statue of the Virgin Mary with child. Sweyn put down his suitcase and pointed to a large room at the left. It was furnished with chairs and tables and there were bookcases filled with books covering two of the walls.

"That is the library and visiting room," Sweyn said. "On the same side down the hall is the dining room and beyond it the kitchen. On the right is Father Rodriguez's office and next to it his bedroom. Then comes the chapel and the bedrooms of the other priests. The stairway at the end of the hall leads up to the classrooms on the second floor and the dormitory on the third floor. Maybe you can sneak up to the washroom and clean up before we see Father Rodriguez."

"It wouldn't do any good," Tom said. "Father O'Malley is sure to mention to him how I look."

"We will leave our suitcases here," Sweyn said. Then he walked over and knocked on a door that had a brass plate on it reading:

FATHER RODRIGUEZ

SUPERINTENDENT

"Come in," a baritone voice called.

If Tom had known what that deep voice had in store for him, he would have taken Sweyn's advice and tried to sneak upstairs. But the trouble was that Tom judged all Jesuit priests by the only priest he knew, Father Joe. His real name was Father Giovanni but nobody could pronounce it right so everybody called him Father Joe. He was known as "the priest on horseback" because he covered such a big territory all over southwestern Utah. Father Joe only came to Adenville once a year for one week. During that week he baptized Catholic babies, married Catholics, and held confessions and masses in the Community Church because we didn't have a Catholic church in Adenville. Father Joe was a regular fellow who smoked cigars and wasn't above taking a nip now and then.

During Father Joe's last visit to Adenville Tom had borrowed books from the priest about the Society of Jesus and spent hours questioning Father Joe. Tom believed he had to know all about the Jesuits because he was going to a Jesuit academy.

He learned that the Society of Jesus was founded in 1534 by Saint Ignatius Loyola and six companions in Paris. They submitted a constitution for the religious order to Pope Paul III in 1540. It was approved a year later

43

and Saint Ignatius was elected general of the order. The society grew in numbers until the 1660s and 1670s, when monarchs jealous of the Jesuits' power suppressed the order in the Spanish dominions and in France. Later Pope Clement XIV dissolved the order and it ceased to exist except in Russia. It was reestablished in 1814 by Pope Pius VII and became the largest religious order in the Catholic church.

The Jesuits distinguished themselves in three fields: their foreign missions, Jesuit schools, and their study of the arts and sciences. They were the first Christian missionaries to live with the American Indians, where they were known as the Black Robes. They preached Christianity and taught many Indian chiefs the French and English languages.

Tom learned that it took sixteen years to become a Jesuit priest. A novice had to spend two years in spiritual training and then take the three vows of chastity, poverty, and obedience. He then became a scholastic. He spent five years studying the arts and sciences, five years teaching, three more years of theological study, and finally another year of spiritual training before he could be ordained a Jesuit priest.

Oh, yes, Tom knew a great deal about the Jesuits. But what he didn't know was that the only resemblance between Father Joe and Father Rodriguez was that both of them were Jesuit priests.

The superintendent was sitting behind a desk in a very sparsely furnished office when Tom entered with Sweyn. The only furniture was the desk and a chair and a large bookcase. There was a large crucifix on the white wall behind the desk and near it a narrow board with a peg, from which hung a ring of keys. There wasn't even a carpet on the floor. Tom began to think that if this was the best they could do for the superintendent, the students must have to sleep on the floor.

Father Rodriguez was a man Tom judged to be about forty-five. The priest was wearing the traditional black robe with the hood pushed to the back of his neck. He had jet-black hair and a swarthy complexion inherited from his Spanish ancestors. But the dominant impression Tom had of the superintendent were the eyes and the face. The eyes were as black as wet coal and the stern face looked as if it would break if the priest smiled.

"Welcome back to the academy, Sweyn," he said in his deep voice. "I see that God has treated you well during your vacation."

"Thank you, Father," Sweyn said. "I am happy to be back. May I present my brother Tom, I mean, Thomas."

Father Rodriguez stared at Tom with those coal-black eyes. "Well, Thomas, what have you to say for yourself?" he asked.

"I guess you mean about the way I look," Tom said. "I rode in the cab of the locomotive from Provo to Salt Lake City. And please, I would rather be called Tom, not Thomas."

If Tom expected the superintendent to react the same way as Father O'Malley, he was as mistaken as a rabbit that challenges a hound dog to a fight.

"We expect our students to be presentable when they arrive," the priest said sternly. "Your punishment for arriving in this condition will be five days of peeling potatoes

in the kitchen. And here at the academy, Thomas, you will be known by the name you were baptized."

Tom didn't think the priest was being fair. It was a great honor to ride in a locomotive. Father Rodriguez acted as if it was no more than riding a horse.

At home Papa always encouraged us boys to speak up if a punishment seemed unfair. So Tom said, "I don't think I should be punished for doing something every kid in the world dreams of doing."

"What you think and what I think are two different matters," Father Rodriguez said sharply. "And your insolence to your superiors is going to cost you five demerits. There is more to getting an education than just putting knowledge in your head. The purpose of this academy is to guide, nourish, and stimulate a boy's mind and heart. And to develop intelligent, spiritually vigorous, cultured, healthy, vocationally prepared, and socially minded American Catholics. And part of that training is to instill in you respect for your elders and superiors."

Did that shut Tom up? Heck no. He was so angry that he didn't use his great brain at all.

"I'm sorry," he said, "but I still don't think it is right to be punished for riding in a locomotive."

"That remark is going to cost you another five demerits," the superintendent said. "We shall tame your tongue and your temper, Thomas, and believe me we shall tame you."

Sweyn tried to put in a word for Tom. "Please, Father," he pleaded, "my brother isn't used to priests. We only saw a missionary priest once a year back home. He really doesn't mean to be disrespectful."

47

"I am aware that your brother has received very little religious instruction," Father Rodriguez said. "But neither did you and we had no trouble at all with you last year. You were a well-behaved and model student."

"Tom is different because he has a great brain," Sweyn said.

"Do you mean he is a precocious child?" Father Rodriguez asked. "That could possibly account for his being temperamental."

Tom didn't like having the priest and Sweyn discuss him as if he weren't even in the room.

"I'm not a child," he said. "I'm almost twelve years old. And I'm just as levelheaded as the next fellow."

The superintendent's eyes seemed to become even darker and the stern face more unyielding as he looked at Tom.

"Your father wrote me that I could expect some trouble with you," he said, to Tom's astonishment. "I will now give you a fair warning, Thomas. If you want to remain here you will obey all the rules and regulations and show proper respect for your elders and superiors. Is that understood?"

"Yes," Tom answered.

"Yes what?" the superintendent asked.

"Yes, Father," Tom said.

Tom admitted he felt completely defeated at that moment. It wasn't due to Father Rodriguez. Just knowing that Papa had so little confidence in him, he felt as if his own flesh and blood had deserted him.

Then the superintendent appeared to relax a little as he leaned back in his chair. "If you have any money you want to turn over to me," he said, "you may do so. There is no place to spend it inside the academy. And one of the rules of the academy is that candy is forbidden except on every fourth Saturday. It is bad for a boy's teeth and health. If you have any candy you must turn it over to me. I will send it to the orphanage."

That was one time Tom sure as heck wanted to say what was on his mind. If candy was bad for the teeth and health of the boys at the academy why wasn't it bad for the kids in the orphanage? But he used his great brain and kept his mouth shut, knowing it would only mean more demerits.

Sweyn said, "I knew better than to bring any candy with me."

Tom knew he couldn't lie to a priest but the candy had cost him sixty cents. His great brain came to the rescue.

"I haven't any candy on me," he said, which was the truth because the candy was in his suitcase and not on his person.

Sweyn looked so startled Tom was afraid our brother would spill the beans. Fortunately the superintendent was looking at him, not at Sweyn.

"You two are the last to arrive," Father Rodriguez said. "Sweyn, you take bunk number ten on the eighth-grade side and show your brother to bunk number ten on the seventh-grade side. You are both excused."

If I had been in Tom's shoes I wouldn't even have unpacked my suitcase. Any fellow who could get ten demerits in about ten minutes was sure to get another ten in a hurry and be expelled.

"It didn't take you long to get Father Rodriguez down on you," Sweyn said when they were in the hallway.

"And you get caught with that candy in your suitcase and you will be expelled for sure."

"You signed a statement not to interfere," Tom said as they picked up their suitcases.

Sweyn just shook his head as they walked down the hallway.

"Want to see the chapel?" he asked.

Tom had never been inside a Catholic church or seen a chapel.

"Sure," he said.

Tom was surprised at how beautiful the chapel was after the austerity of the superintendent's office. The altar was made from stone with a crucifix and a tabernacle to contain the reserved Host in the middle. There were small statues of saints in niches on the walls. On one side of the altar was a statue of the Virgin Mary and on the other a statue of Saint Jude Thaddeus. Next to each was a confessional. And the chapel was one place where there was carpeting in the aisle.

"Don't they have an organ and a choir?" Tom asked.

"They are going to try to raise enough money to buy an organ this year," Sweyn answered. "And Father O'Malley picks just six boys each year for the choir. I'm going to light a candle and say a prayer to Saint Jude for you."

Catholics only prayed to Saint Jude when their troubles seemed hopeless and desperate. Sweyn did the right thing in asking Saint Jude to help Tom. He knew he was going to need all the help the saint could give to prevent The Great Brain from being expelled from the academy.

Right then Tom was feeling pretty hopeless and desperate himself. He had only been in the academy about fifteen minutes and already had received ten demerits and five days of peeling potatoes as punishment. But he didn't want Sweyn to know how he felt. So he knelt in the back row of the chapel and said A Universal Prayer for all Things Necessary to Salvation. It was a good choice in my opinion because part of that prayer was asking God to make Tom always remember to be submissive to his superiors.

They left the chapel and after picking up their suitcases walked up to the second floor.

"The seventh-grade classroom is on the left," Sweyn said, "and the eighth-grade classroom on the right. There is a washroom and a dispensary at the end of the hall. Father Rodriguez takes care of any boy who gets sick."

Then Sweyn put his arm around Tom's shoulders. "As brother to brother, do me and yourself a favor, T.D.," he said, calling Tom by his initials because that is how Papa often addressed us. We all had the same middle name, Dennis, because of a family tradition.

"What favor?" Tom asked.

"Get rid of the candy in your suitcase," Sweyn said. "We can go into the washroom on this floor and open window and throw it down into the street."

"No," Tom said.

"If it is the money you are worrying about," Sweyn said, "I'll give you the sixty cents to get rid of it."

That, for my money, was a darn generous offer for Sweyn to make. But did Tom accept? Heck no. His money-loving heart wouldn't let him.

"Why should I sell the candy to you for sixty cents when there are kids in the dormitory who will give me a dollar and twenty cents for it?" he asked.

That made Sweyn angry, and who could blame him?

To try to save Tom he was willing to hand over a small fortune. "There is a limit to my brotherly love," he said. "If you think that I'm going to let you connive me out of a dollar and twenty cents, you are sadly mistaken, little brother. Go ahead and get yourself expelled. I'm afraid even Saint Jude can't help you."

"Know what your trouble is, S.D.?" Tom said. "Like all people with little brains you worry about things that never happen."

But Tom was going to learn as time passed that even people who have great brains can get into plenty of trouble.

CHAPTER FOUR

Tom's First Day at the Academy

I DON'T KNOW if it was Saint Jude helping out or not but Tom did get through his first day at the academy without any more demerits. His next letter told me all about it.

He and Sweyn walked up to the third floor. There was a statue of Saint Francis in one corner at the end of the hallway. Sweyn told Tom the dormitory and washroom were on the right and there was a big storeroom on the left. The dormitory was a rectangular room with white walls and a bare wooden floor. There were ten beds, ten desks, ten lockers, and ten chairs lined up on each side of the room. On the wall at one end was a colored picture of the Sacred Heart of Jesus and on the wall at the other end a large crucifix.

Several eighth graders who knew Sweyn crowded around to shake hands and say hello. He introduced them to Tom. A boy named Rory Flynn who had dark hair and flashing eyes pointed at Tom's face.

"What happened to you?" he asked. "Did you fall into a coal bin on your way here?" He laughed.

"I rode in the cab of the locomotive from Provo to Salt Lake City," Tom said.

All the kids stared at Tom as if he had just said he'd descended from heaven.

"It's the truth," Sweyn said.

That made Tom a hero. The boys wouldn't even let him go wash up until he had told them all about the ride. Then he went to the washroom with a red-headed seventh grader following him. The boy waited until Tom had cleaned up and then held out his hand.

"My name is Jerry Moran," he said. "I've got bunk number nine, next to you."

They shook hands and then returned to the dormitory. Tom put his suitcase on his bunk and began to unpack. When the kids saw the candy they all crowded around his bunk.

"Didn't you tell your brother bringing candy into the academy is against the rules?" Rory Flynn asked Sweyn.

"I told him," Sweyn said, beginning to unpack his own suitcase.

An eighth grader with a thin face pointed at Tom. "You lied to Father Rodriguez," he said.

Tom walked over and stood in front of the boy. "Nobody calls T.D. Fitzgerald a liar and gets away with it," he said. "You take that back or fight me."

The boy was older and bigger than Tom. But it was as plain as a fly on your nose that he was a coward. His lips began to tremble.

"I'm sorry," he apologized. "I take it back."

Tom accepted the apology and then faced the other kids. "Just so you all understand," he said, "Father Rodriguez asked me if I had any candy. I told him I didn't have any candy on me. I wasn't lying because the candy was in my suitcase."

Rory patted Sweyn on the back. "We'll help your brother eat the candy so he doesn't get into any trouble," he said.

"If any of you kids want a bar of candy," Tom said, "it will cost you a dime."

"But they are only nickel bars of candy," Rory protested.

"That is the price in a store," Tom said. "Ten cents is the price in the academy."

Rory was completely flabbergasted as he stared at Sweyn. "What kind of a brother have you got?" he asked.

"An eighteen-karat conniver," Sweyn answered.

That for my money was a low-down thing for Sweyn to say about his own brother. But he told me he had to do it so that once Tom started swindling them, the kids couldn't say he hadn't warned them.

Rory must have been peeved at not getting a free bar of candy. "Maybe you did put one over on Father Rodriguez," he said. "But smuggling candy into the academy is not only against the rules but also a sin."

Tom knew right then if he expected to open a candy store he had to convince the kids of two things. First that buying candy from him was not a sin. And that having candy and eating it inside the academy wasn't against the rules. His great brain began to work like sixty. He removed his catechism and his Bible from his suitcase and placed them on the bunk. Then he took the three silver dollars from his pocket and put them on the bunk.

"Now put your money where your mouth is, Rory," he said. "I'll bet those three silver dollars against just twenty-five cents of your own money that you can't show me any place in the catechism or the Bible where it says that it is a sin for a fellow to have all the candy he wants in a Catholic academy."

Rory must have known he would lose that bet. "So it isn't a sin," he said. "But it is against the rules."

Tom had expected Rory to say this and already his great brain had figured out an answer. "Sweyn told me all the fellows are allowed to buy ten cents worth of candy once every four weeks," he said. "Is that right?"

Rory and the other kids nodded their heads.

"Now suppose," Tom said, "that each of us bought ten cents worth of licorice sticks and we cut them up into twenty-eight pieces. And every day for twenty-eight days we ate just one piece of the licorice sticks. And when the four weeks were up we bought another ten cents worth of candy and divided it up so we could eat one piece each day until another four weeks passed. And we kept on doing this until school ended. We would be eating candy every day of the school year right here in the academy without breaking any rules. Am I right?"

Tom knew when all the kids began to nod their heads that he had won his argument. "So," he said, "there is no rule against any student eating candy any time he wants."

Jerry Moran took a dime out of his pocket and handed it to Tom. "I'll take one of those bars with peanuts on top," he said.

Tom sold three more bars of candy, including one to Rory Flynn, giving him a profit of twenty cents. He could have sold more but the rest of the kids had turned their money in to the superintendent, knowing they couldn't spend any for four weeks. Tom knew they would all get money from their parents on visiting days or by mail once he got his candy store operating. There wasn't a doubt in his mind that he would make a fortune.

He finished unpacking and then spent the next couple of hours getting acquainted with his fellow seventh graders. He took a liking to three of them for three different reasons. He liked Jerry Moran because he believed the red-headed kid was the sort of fellow who would be game for anything. He liked Phil Martin because there was something about the blond boy that made him feel he could trust Phil implicitly. Tony Colacci was a tall boy with dark hair and a long nose. Tom believed he was a sensitive kid who would value his friendship to the point where he could get the boy to do anything he wanted. The four of them were sitting on Tom's bunk talking when a bell rang.

Sweyn came over and told them that the bell was the signal for everybody to wash up for supper. Tom didn't go to the washroom because he had washed the soot and coal dust from himself after arriving. Anyway he needed this opportunity to hide the candy. He remembered the statue of Saint Francis in the hallway. He waited until all the boys were in the washroom, and then went out in the hall. Saint Francis proved to be a good friend. The statue was set on a hollow base that had an opening in the back. Tom hid the candy there and then returned to the dormitory. He wasn't afraid of anybody stealing the candy. But he was sure that among the ten eighth graders and the other nine seventh graders there had to be at least one tattletale.

When the kids returned to the dormitory Rory Flynn began giving the seventh graders orders.

"All you little seventh graders line up two-by-two in the aisle," he said.

Tom walked over to Sweyn. "What is this all about?" he asked.

"It is called hazing," Sweyn said. "All seventh graders have to go through it for a week. I did last year."

Tom got in line beside Jerry. The eighth graders began to inspect the hands, faces, and necks of the seventh graders.

"Shame on you," Rory said as he looked behind Tom's ears. "You didn't wash behind your ears."

"I did so," Tom said.

"Seventh graders are forbidden to contradict eighth graders during hazing week," Rory said. "Go wash behind your ears."

The eighth graders made all the seventh graders go to the washroom and stood over them to make sure they all washed up again. When they returned to the dormitory they were lined up again.

"Stand at attention and salute the eighth graders," Rory ordered.

Tom stood at attention with his fellow seventh graders until the supper bell finally rang.

"At ease," Rory said. "You may go down to the dining room now."

The dining room had a long wooden table with benches. There were a tin bowl, a tin plate, a tin cup, a napkin, and a knife, fork, and spoon for each student. Father Rodriguez was sitting on a high stool at the head of the table. He waited until all the seventh graders were standing on one side of the table and eighth graders on the other side.

"You may sit down now," he said. "But there will be no talking. For the benefit of you new boys it is our custom to assign two seventh graders and two eighth graders for kitchen and dining-room duty each week. These four students will be excused from morning prayer and will report to Father Petrie at six thirty each morning. I will now call out the names of the first four boys in alphabetical order: Harold Adams, Peter Brennan, John Burton, and Frank Carver. You four boys will remain after supper to help Father Petrie wash and dry the dishes and perform any other duties he may assign to you. For this one meal only Father O'Malley and Father Wegland will serve you."

The two priests came out of the kitchen carrying large buckets with ladles in them. Father Wegland was a tall, thin-faced man who walked with a slight limp. Tom learned later that the priest had a club foot. They filled the tin bowls with vegetable soup. Two seventh graders grabbed their spoons and were about to start eating.

"You will not start to eat until I have said grace," Father Rodriguez said.

Tom had to wait until Father O'Malley and Father Wegland filled the tin cups with milk, gave each boy two slices of bread, filled the tin plates with ham hocks and lima beans, and placed two sugar cookies by each boy's plate. Not until then did Father Rodriguez say Grace Before Meals.

Tom couldn't honestly say the food was bad. He was used to Mamma's and Aunt Bertha's cooking and compared to theirs the food was bad. The soup was almost cold by the time he could eat it. And by the time he'd finished the soup, the ham hocks and lima beans were no longer warm. But he had to admit the sugar cookies were delicious.

When the meal was over Father Rodriguez said Grace After Meals and excused all but the four boys he'd named for kitchen and dining-room duty. The eighth graders had entered the dining room last and were the first to leave. Sweyn was waiting for Tom at the foot of the stairway.

"That kid Willie Connors who said you lied dropped out of line," Sweyn said. "He is going to snitch on you so you had better get rid of that candy."

"Let him snitch," Tom said as they started up the stairway. "My great brain is a long way ahead of Willie Connors." Then he changed the subject. "You never told me the kids have to work like dogs here even when they aren't being punished. Our parents pay to send us here and Father Rodriguez expects us to do all the work."

"Don't be silly," Sweyn said. "There isn't a priest here who doesn't put in at least fourteen hours a day. Father Petrie does all the marketing and cooking and teaches when one of the other priests is ill. Father Wegland teaches and does all the carpentry and all the laundry and sewing for the kids as well as the priests. Father O'Malley teaches all day and takes care of the grounds outside and is the barber for all the fellows. Father Rodriguez teaches in addition to doing all the clerical and bookkeeping work himself and running the academy. If anybody works like a dog around here it is the Jesuit priests."

Tom admitted that made him feel ashamed. "I didn't know all that," he said.

Upstairs Tom sat on his bunk talking with Jerry, Phil, and Tony. In a few minutes Willie Connors entered the dormitory. About five minutes later Father Rodriguez arrived.

"Stand at the foot of your bunks for inspection," the superintendent ordered.

Tom couldn't help but smile as he watched the priest make a rapid inspection of the lockers, desks, and suitcases of the other students. But when Father Rodriguez came to Tom's bunk the priest made a very thorough search of everything, even pulling down the bed clothes and looking under the mattress. And then he searched Tom personally. Father Rodriguez looked even more mystified than the kids when he didn't find any candy.

As he walked out of the dormitory Jerry patted Tom on the back. "You sure put one over on Father Rodriguez," he said.

"You mean on Willie Connors," Tom said as he started walking toward the snitcher's bunk.

Willie backed up against the wall, looking as frightened as a mouse cornered by a tomcat. "You hit me and I'll tell Father Rodriguez," he cried.

"I'm not going to hit you, Willie," he said. "That would be letting you off too easy." Then Tom turned to face the other fellows. "I'm going to cure him of being a tattletale. That way we won't have to worry about him snitching on us for the rest of the school year."

"You can't cure him," Rory said. "He snitched on everybody all last year."

"We have a cure for a tattletale back home," Tom said. "It's called the silent treatment. That means none of us will speak to Willie and if he speaks to us we'll just pretend we don't hear him. We won't have anything to do with Willie Connors the snitcher. If we all give him the silent treatment for a week maybe that will cure him. If not, we will give him the silent treatment for the rest of the school year. Are you with me, fellows?"

The rest of the seventh and eighth graders all pledged to give Willie the silent treatment.

"I won't snitch anymore!" Willie cried. "I promise."

Tom looked at the other fellows. "I didn't hear anything," he said. "Did any of you fellows?"

They all shook their heads. The silent treatment for Willie had begun.

At seven thirty a bell rang. Sweyn came over to Tom's bunk. "That is the bell for Saturday night confessions," he said. "You seventh graders use the confessional on the right side of the altar and we use the one on the left."

Tom marched down to the chapel and sat down on the right side with the seventh graders. He was plenty worried when it came his turn to enter the confessional. It would be just his luck for Father Rodriguez to hear his confession. He said the Act of Contrition. Then he decided he had to know which priest was hearing his confession.

"Father Rodriguez?" he asked.

"Why do you ask, my son?" a voice he recognized as belonging to Father O'Malley asked.

"Well," Tom said, "what might be called a sin by Father Rodriguez wouldn't be called a sin by Father Joe, who heard my last confession."

"A sin is a sin," Father O'Malley said. "Can you explain exactly what you mean?"

"I know it is a sin to be angry at anyone or to strike anyone," Tom said, "but you take a fellow like Sammy Leeds back home. He is a bully. I had to give him a whipping since my last confession for picking on a smaller boy. I know Jesus taught we should turn the other cheek. But you turn the other cheek to a fellow like Sammy and he'll paste you one on it. Father Joe understood about Sammy and never gave me any penance for fighting him."

"Go on, my son," Father O'Malley said.

"I know it is a sin to tell a lie," Tom said, "but it all depends on what you call a lie. I exaggerated a little bit to put over some deals. Father Joe never gave me any penance for that either. But he always caught me on one sin. I'm proud of my great brain and I guess I'm vain about it. Father Joe said that was a sin. But I think anybody who has a great brain has a right to be proud of it."

"Heaven help us," Father O'Malley said. "A doubting Thomas. You are aptly named."

"I know that I have committed one great sin," Tom said. "I've broken the fourth commandment, which forbids all disobedience, contempt, and stubbornness toward our parents or superiors, and which commands us to honor and obey our bishops, pastors, magistrates, teachers, and other lawful superiors. I don't think I can honor Father Rodriguez because I don't like him and how can you honor somebody you don't like? And that is the only real sin I can think of since my last confession."

Father O'Malley's voice became filled with stern authority. "Your confession has been blasphemous," he said. "I realize your religious instruction has been wanting but that is no excuse for such conduct. I will now give you penance. In addition to your usual prayers you will say an Act of Faith, an Act of Hope, an Act of Love, the Hail Mary, the Apostles' Creed, the Confiteor and an Act of Contrition on your knees in the chapel every day until your next confession. Go now, my son, and may God help you."

Tom had got through his first day at the academy without getting any more demerits. But he sure made up for it by receiving more penance than he had received in a lifetime from Father Joe. And as he left the confessional he couldn't help thinking how different these city priests were.

At the rate Tom was going he wouldn't have time to get an education at the academy because he would be spending most of his time doing penance.

CHAPTER FIVE

From Bad to Worse

I KNEW FROM READING Tom's next letter that he was going from bad to worse at the academy. At the rate he was going we could expect him to be sent home any day.

Tom thought he was dreaming his first Sunday morning when Father Rodriguez woke him up. It was still pitch dark in the dormitory.

"Get dressed quietly so you don't wake up the other boys," the superintendent said.

"But it is the middle of the night," Tom protested.

"It is exactly four o'clock in the morning," Father Rodriguez said.

66

Tom couldn't imagine where they were going at that hour as he followed the priest down the stairway. The superintendent had threatened to tame him. Maybe he was being taken down to be locked up in a dungeon. Instead he was taken to the kitchen. Father Rodriguez turned on the electric lights and showed Tom a drawer where paring knives were kept. Then he pointed at a sack of potatoes and a wooden tub half filled with water.

"Every night Father Petrie will set out the number of potatoes he wants peeled for the next day's meals," the superintendent said. "You will peel those potatoes and drop them into the tub of water. You will be doing this for five mornings so I suggest that you go to bed at night before lights-out. Father Petrie will come into the kitchen at five o'clock to build up the fire in the range and start preparing breakfast. It usually takes a boy about two hours to peel the potatoes needed each day. You should be finished when the six o'clock bell rings."

If there was one thing Tom hated to do it was to peel spuds. Whenever Mamma or Aunt Bertha was sick one of us boys had to peel potatoes. When it was Tom's turn he always paid me to do it for him. So I can imagine how he felt as he stared at all those spuds.

"You are making me break the third commandment, which forbids all unnecessary servile work on Sundays," he said seriously.

But Father Rodriguez wasn't worrying about breaking a commandment. "The good Lord knows that people must eat on the sabbath," he said. "I shall return at six o'clock."

Tom stood staring at the sack of potatoes after the priest had left. He asked himself why a fellow with a great brain should have to peel all those spuds. So instead of starting to work he sat down and put his great brain to work. In less than a minute he had the answer to his problem. If it took one boy two hours to peel all those potatoes four boys could do it in half an hour.

He had noticed coming downstairs that the stairs squeaked. He sneaked back up to the dormitory, walking close to the banister so there weren't any squeaks. He woke up Jerry, Phil, and Tony and held a whispered conversation with them on his bunk.

"You fellows know that sooner or later you'll get caught doing something and have to peel spuds," he said. "You help me and I'll help you when the time comes."

Jerry nodded his head. "I'll help," he said.

Tom was right about Jerry. The red-headed kid was game for anything. But Phil wasn't.

"Not me," Phil said. "If we get caught we'll all end up with demerits."

"Me neither," Tony said. "Go peel your own spuds."

"Come on, Tom," Jerry said. "I'll help you. Let these two 'fraidy cats go back to bed."

That made Phil angry. "I'm no 'fraidy cat," he said.

"Then prove it," Jerry said.

"All right, I'll help," Phil said.

The three of them looked at Tony.

"Haw," Tony said.

They all stared at Tony for a moment. Finally Tom spoke.

"What do you mean by 'haw'?" he asked. "Do you mean ha like in 'ha, ha,' or haw like telling a horse to turn left, or what?"

"I don't know," Tony said.

68

"What do you mean you don't know?" Tom asked. "You just said it."

"When my father has an argument with my mother or my uncle," Tony said, "and he doesn't know what to say he always says 'haw.'"

"In other words, you don't know what to say," Tom said. "Well, all you've got to say is 'I am not a 'fraidy cat' or 'I am a 'fraidy cat.'"

"I'll help," Tony said.

They all slid down the banister to the ground floor and then tiptoed into the kitchen. Tom showed them where the paring knives were kept. Thirty minutes later all the potatoes were peeled and Jerry, Phil, and Tony were upstairs in the dormitory. Tom was sitting there doing nothing when Father Petrie entered the kitchen at five o'clock.

The priest was a short, very fat man with big jowls. He placed the palms of his hands on his fat belly and looked at Tom with twinkling eyes.

"Bless my soul," he said, his jowls wobbling as he spoke. "You must be Thomas Fitzgerald."

"Yes, Father," Tom said.

The priest walked over and looked at the tub containing all the peeled potatoes. "Bless my soul, Thomas," he said, "you couldn't possibly have peeled all those potatoes in an hour."

Father Petrie left the kitchen shaking his head. He returned in a few minutes with Father Rodriguez.

"You must have awakened the boy before four o'clock," Father Petrie said.

The superintendent stared at the tub of peeled potatoes. "There is no other logical explanation," he said.

Then he looked at Tom. "You are excused for now, Thomas."

Tom went up to the dormitory where Jerry, Phil, and Tony were waiting on Jerry's bunk. He told them what had happened. They all laughed so much they had to hold their hands over their mouths.

"We've got Father Rodriguez and Father Petrie plumb mystified," Tom said before they all went to bed.

The six o'clock bell woke them up. All the boys washed up and changed into their Sunday clothes. Then two eighth graders left to serve as altar boys. At six thirty another bell rang and Tom went with the others down to the chapel for mass. Then they went to the dining room for breakfast before going back to the dormitory.

"My folks are coming to see me today," Phil said.

Jerry shook his head. "I wish my folks lived in Salt Lake City so they could visit me," he said.

"That reminds me," Tom said. "I've still got eight bars of candy." Then he stood up. "You fellows who are having visitors today, don't forget to ask for money if you want any candy."

All the kids had ignored Willie Connors and I guess the silent treatment was hurting him. He came over to Tom's bunk.

"I said I was sorry," he said. "And I promise not to snitch anymore."

Tom and the other fellows pretended not to hear. Willie went back to his bunk and began to cry.

Tom was sitting on a bench with Jerry and Tony in the yard that afternoon when Sweyn came over to them.

"Father Rodriguez just sent for me," he said. "He asked me where you had learned how to peel potatoes so fast. I told him you had never peeled a potato before in your life. You always hired J.D. to do it when Mom or Aunt Bertha was sick."

"Why couldn't you keep your mouth shut?" Tom said, plenty angry. "You signed a statement not to interfere. Now you are going to have to help me because I'll need a lookout."

"I don't know what you are talking about," Sweyn said, "but whatever it is the answer is no."

Tom shrugged as if he didn't care. "Then I guess I'll have to tell all the kids you refused to help your own brother," he said. "And I'll also tell them you can't be trusted because you broke your signed statement."

Poor Sweyn knew he was trapped. By the time Tom got through telling it the kids would have more respect for Willie Connors than for him.

"All right, you little blackmailer," he said. "What do you want me to do?"

"I'll tell you after supper tonight," Tom said. "My great brain has to work on it a little longer."

After visiting hours were over Tom sold six bars of candy. And because he didn't want the other two bars to go stale he divided them up with his three friends.

Father Rodriguez woke up Tom at four o'clock again the next morning. Tom waited until the priest had left the kitchen and then sneaked up to the dormitory. He woke up his three friends and Sweyn. They all slid down the banister to the ground floor.

"Father Rodriguez has to come through the dining room to get to the kitchen," Tom whispered. "S.D., you station yourself just inside the entrance to the dining room where you can see the door of his bedroom. I have a hunch Father Rodriguez will be checking on me this morning. If you see him open his bedroom door you run into the kitchen and tell us. Then the four of you hide in the pantry until he is gone."

Tom's hunch was right. He and his three friends had only been peeling potatoes for fifteen minutes when Sweyn came running into the kitchen.

"He's coming," Sweyn whispered.

Tom was sitting all alone in the kitchen with a potato in one hand and a paring knife in the other when the superintendent entered the kitchen.

"Did you want something, Father?" Tom asked as innocent as could be.

The superintendent looked at the peeled potatoes in the wooden tub. He didn't say a word but walked out of the kitchen shaking his head. He paid another visit to the kitchen fifteen minutes later. Again the four boys hid in the pantry and Tom greeted the superintendent with a big innocent smile.

Father Rodriguez didn't return to the kitchen until five o'clock. Father Petrie was with him. By that time all the spuds were peeled and Jerry, Phil, Tony, and Sweyn were back in the dormitory.

"I know for a fact," the superintendent said to Father Petrie, "that I didn't make a mistake about the time this morning. I checked my alarm clock with my watch and also with the clock in the library. And I checked on Thomas twice."

"Bless my soul," Father Petrie said, placing the palms of his hands on his belly. "There is only one logical conclusion. Thomas is without a doubt the fastest potato peeler in the world."

73

The superintendent just shook his head. "You are excused, Thomas," he said.

Tom was chuckling all the way back to the dormitory. His three friends were waiting on Jerry's bunk.

"Father Rodriguez will rue the day he sentenced me to peeling spuds for just riding on a locomotive," Tom said. "And he'll be sorry he ever tangled with my great brain."

Jerry shook his head. "Wish we could tell all the kids about the good joke we played on him," he said. "None of the kids like him except maybe Willie Connors."

"We can't tell anybody," Tom said, "or the next kid sentenced to peeling spuds will do the same thing."

Tom began his first day of school that Monday morning. His life was controlled by the big bell on the ground floor. The six o'clock bell was the signal for all the boys to get washed up and dressed. Then the four kids assigned to the dining room and kitchen left. The six-thirty bell called the boys to chapel for morning prayer. Another bell sent them from the chapel to the dining room. From the dining room they went back to the dormitory. At eight o'clock the sound of another bell sent them to the classrooms on the second floor.

Father Rodriguez was standing in front of the blackboard in the seventh-grade classroom. He assigned each seventh grader to a desk.

"You will find textbooks for the courses Father O'Malley will teach you on your desks," he said. "You will be studying beginner's Latin, geography, American history, advanced arithmetic, English grammar, general science, and beginner's civics. You will also find a book entitled *Key of Heaven*, which is a manual of prayers and instruction for Catholics. I will teach this course, which embraces the catechism, epistles and gospels, and Christian doctrine. It will be your first course each day."

Tom discovered that there was no such thing as recess at the academy. Students remained in the classrooms from eight o'clock to twelve noon. They had forty-five minutes for lunch and then went back to the classrooms until three o'clock. Father O'Malley told the seventh graders they could do their homework between the time school let out and suppertime and between seven and nine o'clock in the evenings. And he gave them homework to do for every course.

But there sure as heck wasn't any homework done that afternoon. It was initiation day for the seventh graders. Rory Flynn addressed them as soon as they arrived in the dormitory.

"You little seventh graders have been found guilty of wanting to go to school at the academy," he said. "The punishment is a trip through the torture tunnel."

Then the eighth graders each got a textbook and stood with their legs apart in the aisle. Willie Connors got in line with them but he wasn't there for long. Rory grabbed the tattletale and without a word marched him back to his bunk. Then he got back in line.

"The torture tunnel is ready," he said. "All you little seventh graders get down on your hands and knees and crawl through one at a time."

Tom didn't like having Rory giving him orders. "What if we refuse?" he asked.

Sweyn looked at him. "Don't be a spoilsport," he said.

Tom sure as heck didn't want the fellows to think he was a spoilsport. "I'll go first," he said.

He got down on his hands and knees and began crawling between the legs of the eighth graders. Each one whacked him on the rump with a textbook. Jerry came next. And then one by one the rest of the seventh graders crawled through the torture tunnel. Fun was fun but Tom thought some of the eighth graders, especially Rory, could have taken it a little easier. Three of his classmates had tears in their eyes as they came out of the torture tunnel.

If Tom thought that was the end of the initiation he was mistaken. Rory put a chair at one end of the dormitory and sat down on it.

"We will now prove that all seventh graders are dummies," he said. "Line up and come one at a time to sit on my lap."

All the seventh graders looked at Tom as if expecting him to go first. He walked over and sat on Rory's lap, wondering what this was all about. He didn't have to wonder for long. Rory grabbed hold of the back of his neck as if Tom was a ventriloquist's dummy.

"I've got a dummy on my lap who thinks he is a rooster," Rory said. "Crow like a rooster, dummy."

"Cock-a-doodle-doo!" Tom pretended to crow like a rooster, as both eighth and seventh graders laughed.

Jerry was next on Rory's lap.

"I've got a dummy who thinks he is a cat," Rory said. "Show me you are a cat, dummy."

"Me-ow, me-ow," Jerry said.

One by one the other seventh graders had to sit on Rory's lap. He made them bark like a dog, moo like a cow, whinny like a horse, caw like a crow, roar like a lion, croak like a frog, cry like a baby, and howl like a wolf.

Then Rory stood up. "I guess that proves that all little seventh graders are dummies," he said. "Os habent, et non loquentur."

Sweyn laughed. "Oculos habent, et non videbunt," he said.

Billy Daniels nodded his head. "Ares habent, et non audient," he said.

"And," Larry Williams said, "Nares habent, et non odorabunt."

Then all the eighth graders began to laugh like all get out.

"And don't forget, fellows," Rory said, "when we want to say something we don't want these little seventh graders to know about, all we have to do is to speak in Latin."

Tom didn't like the idea of anybody saying anything he couldn't understand. He walked over to Sweyn.

"What did you fellows say in Latin?" he asked.

"After proving all seventh graders are dummies," Sweyn said, "Rory said they have mouths and speak not. I said they have eyes and see not. Billy said they have ears and hear not. And Larry said they have noses and smell not. But don't ask me to translate any more Latin for you. Like Rory said, when we want to say something to each other we don't want you seventh graders to understand, we will speak in Latin."

Tom admitted this was one time when even his great brain couldn't help him. He knew he couldn't learn Latin any faster than Father O'Malley taught it to him. Sweyn told him that was the end of the initiation but seventh graders would be forced to wash up twice and stand at attention in the mornings for the rest of the week.

It was a good thing Tom had a great brain. There was

no time to do any homework before supper. And after supper he had to spend almost an hour in the chapel doing the penance Father O'Malley had given him. This left him just one hour to do all his homework.

During his third and fourth mornings of peeling spuds Tom was surprised that Father Rodriguez didn't come to check on him. But he got an even bigger surprise on his fifth and last day. When he and the superintendent arrived in the kitchen at four o'clock that morning he found Father Petrie waiting for them.

"This morning, Thomas," Father Rodriguez said, "you are going to have an audience. Father Petrie and I are going to sit right here and watch you peel all those potatoes in less than an hour."

Tom knew he was cornered and only his great brain could save him. But how? He mustn't show any surprise. He had to convince the priests that he alone had peeled all the potatoes on the other four mornings and at the same time get out of peeling them this morning. His great brain came to his rescue.

"First I have to hypnotize myself," he said.

Father Rodriguez stared at him. "Hypnotize yourself?" he asked.

"Bless my soul," Father Petrie said, "you look as if you mean it, Thomas."

Tom put his index fingers to his temples and shut his eyes. He began rocking back and forth.

"I am the fastest potato peeler in the world," he chanted softly. "I am the fastest potato peeler in the world."

He kept saying this over and over until his great brain

gave him the solution to his problem. He dropped his arms and opened his eyes.

"I must get a paring knife now," he said.

To get the knife he had to walk around the sack of potatoes. He made certain it was obvious to both priests that he stubbed his toe on the sack of potatoes. He fell to the floor bracing his fall with his hands. He lay there quietly until the two priests turned him over on his back. Then he blinked his eyes several times.

"What am I doing lying on the floor?" he asked. Then he took hold of his left wrist with his right hand and bit his lip as if in pain. "My wrist hurts. It feels as if I sprained it."

"Bless my soul," Father Petrie said. "Self-hypnosis in a mere boy. I just can't believe it, although you did tell me that Thomas had what he called a great brain."

Both priests helped Tom to his feet and Father Rodriguez examined the wrist.

"I don't see any swelling," Father Rodriguez said.

"Maybe it is just a twisted muscle," Tom said. "I twisted my ankle one time and it didn't swell up. But I couldn't step on it for hours." Tom wasn't lying about his ankle. It really had happened.

"Come with me to the dispensary," the superintendent said.

Tom followed the priest up to the second floor. Father Rodriguez turned on the light in the dispensary. The room contained two beds, a table, and a cabinet holding gauze, bandages, scissors, cans of salves, and other medical supplies.

The superintendent nodded toward a washbasin in the corner. "Let cold water run on your wrist," he said.

Tom did as he was told while the priest opened the cabinet and removed a roll of gauze and a pair of scissors.

"Dry your wrist now with a towel," he said. "I'll bandage it loosely. And if it starts to swell or your fingers start feeling numb, you come see me."

Tom pretended it was painful as he opened and shut his fingers. "I doubt if I could hold a potato in my left hand let alone peel it now," he said.

"I have no intention of forcing you to peel potatoes with a sprained wrist," Father Rodriguez said. "You can return to bed as soon as I bandage it. Father Petrie and I will take care of the potatoes."

A few minutes later Tom entered the dormitory. It was too good a joke to wait until the six o'clock bell, so he awakened Jerry, Phil, and Tony and told them what had happened.

"And right now," he said as he finished, "Father Rodriguez and Father Petrie are peeling spuds in the kitchen."

They all had a good laugh and then went back to bed.

Father Rodriguez conducted the first class that morning as usual. Five minutes before the period ended he made a surprise announcement.

"You will all now hold out your right hands so that I may inspect them," he said.

Tom knew he was caught as he watched the superintendent inspect the fingers of each boy's right hand. The inspection ended just as Father O'Malley entered the classroom to take over as teacher for the rest of the day.

"The following boys," Father Rodriguez said, "will accompany me to my office: Thomas Fitzgerald, Jeremiah

Moran, Phillip Martin and Anthony Colacci."

They followed the priest down to the superintendent's office on the ground floor. Father Rodriguez sat down at his desk.

"I admit, Thomas," he said, "that your remarkable skill in peeling potatoes had me completely baffled. Then this morning I made a discovery. While helping Father Petrie peel potatoes I noticed that the work leaves telltale marks from the paring knife on the thumb and index finger of the right hand."

"I take all the blame," Tom said. "I talked Jerry, Phil, and Tony into helping me."

"That is very noble of you, Thomas," Father Rodriguez said, "but a person who participates in a conspiracy is just as guilty as the ringleader."

Tom was determined to try to save his friends. "If I had never come to the academy," he said, "they wouldn't be in trouble right now."

"You plead like the devil's advocate," the priest said. "But you did come. However, you do have a point. The punishment for your three conspirators should be lighter than your own. And since you have made expert potato peelers out of them, they will peel potatoes for the next three weeks. Jeremiah will take the first week, Phillip the second week, and Anthony the third week."

Tom heard his three friends groan as the sentence was pronounced.

"As for you, Thomas," Father Rodriguez said, "beginning tomorrow you will clean the dormitory washroom between seven thirty and eight o'clock in the evening on Mondays through Fridays and during the afternoon on Saturdays and Sundays. And make no mistake about it, I want that washroom really cleaned. You will scrub the washbasins, shower room, and toilets and mop the floor daily. And that will be your assignment until you go for an entire month without getting any demerits. In addition each of you will receive five demerits. And may I remind you, Thomas, this makes fifteen demerits for you this month. You may all return to your classroom now."

Jerry took the punishment like the good sport he was. "It could have been worse," he said as they climbed the stairs.

Phil was shaking his head. "I told you we would get in trouble," he said. "And that stuff you gave us about you helping us, Tom, was just stuff. Father Rodriguez is going to make sure we don't get any help peeling spuds— even if he has to sit there and watch us. You sure got us into a mess. Don't come to me with any more of your bright ideas."

"That goes for me too," Tony said.

"But fellows," Tom pleaded, "I thought you were my friends. You don't hear Jerry crying, do you? What good is a friend if he deserts you the first time there is a little trouble?"

"Well," Phil said, "when you put it that way I guess I'm still your friend."

"Me too," Tony said.

"You won't regret it," Tom said, "because my great brain has finally figured out a way to get rid of Father Rodriguez."

Tom couldn't have caused more astonishment if he'd said he was going to murder the superintendent. His three friends stared at him bug-eyed. Jerry was the first to recover enough to speak.

"And just how are you going to do that?" he asked.

Tom's idea had come to him so suddenly that he knew his great brain must have been subconsciously working on it since his first day at the academy.

"I'm going to write a letter to the Pope," Tom said. "I'm going to tell him that Father Rodriguez is running this place like a reform school. When I get through telling Pope Leo what is going on around here I'll bet he and the general will excommunicate Father Rodriguez."

Jerry stared at Tom. "Who is the general?" he asked.

"The head of the Society of Jesus is called the general," Tom explained. "But the general and all Jesuits have to take a special vow of obedience to the Pope. And when Pope Leo tells the general to get rid of Father Rodriguez you can bet the general will do it."

Phil was shaking his head. "Don't you have to get permission or something before you can write a letter to the Pope?" he asked.

"I'll explain to Pope Leo in the letter," Tom said, "that I sure as heck can't get permission from Father Rodriguez."

Tony still had his doubts. "If Father Rodriguez sees a letter going out of here from you to the Pope," he said, "he will make you let him read it first."

"I never thought about that," Tom said.

Phil said, "Daniel could mail it."

"Who is Daniel?" Tom asked.

"My older brother," Phil said. "He comes to visit me with our mother and father every Sunday."

"That does it," Tom said grinning. "Pope Leo is going to get an earful about this place and how Father Rodriguez is running it."

CHAPTER SIX

The Academy Candy Store

I PERSONALLY DIDN'T BELIEVE Tom would last another month at the academy after getting fifteen demerits his first month. And I knew things must be pretty tough for Tom when he wrote me about having to peel spuds and clean the washroom. So tough that he had even written a letter to the Pope to complain.

But I didn't have any time right then to think about Tom and his troubles, because I had troubles of my own, and his name was Frankie Pennyworth. He was a four-year-old boy whose parents and brother had been killed in a land slide in Red Rock Canyon. Uncle Mark couldn't find any relatives, so Papa and Mamma had adopted

Frankie. Having a foster brother was sure keeping me busy.

Frankie was a real take-over kid. Tom used to swindle me out of my things. But not Frankie. He just took them. I guess he figured that now that he was a member of the family, anything the family owned he owned. Whatever he wanted of mine he would just take. Then he would look at me with those big dark eyes of his and say, "My wagon," or whatever it was he wanted. He even took my pup Prince this way. I had to borrow my own slingshot from Frankie when I wanted to use it. But I'll admit that he was generous. Anything I used to own that he now owned he would let me borrow. If you are wondering why I didn't put up a fight, there were two reasons. Papa said I must humor Frankie because of the great shock the boy had in losing his own family. And having a younger brother to play with and love was worth everything Frankie took from me.

All I can say is that it was a good thing Tom had a great brain or he wouldn't have even been able to get passing grades. Between doing the heavy penance Father O'Malley kept giving him and having to clean the washroom, Tom didn't have much time left in which to do his homework. And unlike Mr. Standish in Adenville, the Jesuit teachers made a fellow do homework on every subject every day.

Tom sure hated cleaning the washroom. He tried to hire other kids to do it for him. But they hated the work as much as he did and nobody would take on the job. Tom knew if he didn't go for an entire month without getting any demerits that he might be stuck cleaning the washroom until school let out in the spring. Boy, oh, boy, what a revolting thought that was for my brother.

To help take his mind off this degrading job he put his great brain to work on how to get his candy store started. He thought of several plans but had to discard them. He thought of having Phil's brother Daniel buy candy and throw it over the rock wall. But what if one of the priests found it before he did? And he thought about sneaking out of the academy at night and climbing over the big iron gate. He knew he couldn't get over the high rock wall. But when he found out Father O'Malley had insomnia and walked around outside in the yard part of the night he rejected that idea. But did Tom give up? Heck no. He was sure his great brain would solve the problem sooner or later.

One week after the silent treatment had begun, Willie Connors came over to Tom's bunk. Willie sure must have suffered because Sweyn, who had the bunk next to him, had told Tom that Willie cried himself to sleep at night.

"The week is up," Willie said to Tom, "and I haven't snitched on anybody."

Tom was sitting on his bunk with his three friends. "That is right," he said.

"It has been terrible," Willie said. He looked as if he was going to start crying just at the memory of it. "I promise I'll never snitch again."

Tom stood up. "All you fellows listen," he said. "We can lift the silent treatment from Willie because he hasn't snitched on anybody for a week. And Willie knows if he does snitch in the future that we will impose the silent treatment on him until school lets out."

I guess Willie wanted to make sure the silent treatment was ended. He walked around the dormitory speaking to each boy just to make sure they spoke to him.

That evening Father O'Malley again heard Tom's confession. And again the priest imposed a heavy penance because Tom insisted he couldn't honor somebody he didn't like.

The next day Tom gave Phil his letter to the Pope along with fifty cents.

"I know it doesn't cost fifty cents to mail a letter to Italy," he said. "Tell your brother Daniel he can keep the change."

It just goes to prove how much faith Tom had that the Pope and the general would get rid of Father Rodriguez. Tom parting with fifty cents was like a bird parting with its wings.

It wasn't until the following Tuesday evening that Tom's great brain gave him his first idea for getting his candy store started. He always locked the door of the washroom from the inside when he cleaned it so the kids wouldn't walk on the floor before it was dry. The fellows all knew they were supposed to use the washroom on the second floor between seven thirty and eight o'clock.

On this particular night Tom found himself staring at the trapdoor in the washroom ceiling. He knew his great brain was trying to tell him something. He stood on a washbasin and lifted up the trapdoor. Then he hoisted himself up into the attic. The ceiling was high enough for him to stand erect. He walked over to one of the dormer windows and looked down into the street. This was the side of the academy that was flush up against the sidewalk. There was a manufacturing plant and a warehouse across the street, but both were closed at this time in the evening. Tom knew his great brain had given him the solution of how to get in and out of the academy without anybody knowing it. All he needed was a rope long enough to reach the street. Going down wouldn't be any problem but coming up might. It was a long, long way for a fellow to lift himself hand-over-hand.

He went to bed that night trying to think of a way to make it easier to get from the street to the attic. The next morning while he was tying his shoelaces the answer came to him. If he put knots in the rope about two feet apart he could use it like a sort of rope ladder. He could straddle a knot in the rope with his feet and use his arms to hoist himself up another two feet. Then all he had to do was grab another knot and lift himself another two feet. By using his arms and then his legs it would be easy to climb that distance.

His great brain had solved one problem only to leave him with a bigger one. How could he get the rope into the attic? He knew Phil could get his brother Daniel to buy the rope. But if Daniel just threw it over the wall one of the priests might find it. He put his great brain to work again.

The next afternoon when school was out Tom was sitting with his three friends under a tree on the grounds. Jerry had a piece of string. He was showing them how to tie some sailor knots. Jerry's uncle was a sailor and had visited the family the summer before.

"Where did you get that string?" Tom asked.

"In the kitchen," Jerry said. "Father Petrie saves all the string that is wrapped around deliveries from the meat market and grocery store. When I was peeling spuds this morning I asked him for a piece."

Phil's face was sad. "Your week of peeling spuds will soon be over," he said. "Then comes my week."

"And after that comes my week," added Tony mournfully.

"Forget about peeling spuds," Tom said. "My great brain has got almost everything figured out about starting my candy store. Jerry, tomorrow morning before Father Petrie comes into the kitchen you get me about fifty feet of the strongest string he has."

"What are you going to do with it?" Jerry asked.

"I'll tell you all about it Saturday," Tom said. "I want to give my great brain time to make sure the plan is perfect."

Tom's money-loving heart didn't like what his great brain kept telling him. He knew he couldn't operate his candy store without the help of his three friends. And to Tom giving up part of the profits was the same as a man lost on the desert giving up his last canteen of water. But he knew there was no alternative.

On Saturday he met with his three friends under the tree in the yard. "We will now form the Academy Candy Store Corporation," he announced.

Jerry, Phil, and Tony looked at him as if he had just announced they were going to blow up the academy with dynamite.

"First we will need a president," Tom said. "And due to the fact that it is my great brain's idea and I am going to finance the corporation, I will be president."

Jerry finally recovered from his astonishment. "What does that make us?" he asked.

"Stockholders in the corporation," Tom answered.

"And as stockholders you will each be entitled to ten per cent of the profits."

"Now you are talking," Jerry said with a grin.

Tom took out two of the silver dollars he had got from the poker players on the train and handed them to Phil.

"When your family comes to visit you tomorrow," he said, "you get Daniel to one side and slip him this money. Tell him to buy fifty feet of one-inch manila rope. It shouldn't cost more than two or three cents a foot. He can keep the change if he will do what you tell him."

"Which is what?" Phil asked.

"To bring the rope to the side of the academy where it is flush up against the sidewalk," Tom said. "He must arrive at exactly seven thirty Monday evening. Tell him I will be at the attic window directly above the third-floor washroom. I will tie a rock on the end of the string Jerry got for me and let it down. All Daniel has to do is tie the string to one end of the rope so I can pull the rope up to the attic. Got it?"

"Got it," Phil said.

Monday evening at seven twenty-five Tom made his usual announcement. "You fellows are going to have to use the washroom on the second floor for the next half hour."

Then he went inside the washroom and locked the door. He climbed through the trapdoor to the attic and opened the dormer window. In a couple of minutes he saw Daniel coming down the street. Jerry had doubted Daniel would cooperate. But Tom didn't have any doubts after learning Daniel had spent two years at the academy and stood to make fifty cents besides.

Tom let down the string with the rock tied to it. He watched Daniel remove the rock and tie the string to one end of the rope. Then he hauled it up, coiled it on the floor, and returned to the washroom. He did his cleaning job and then joined his three friends on Jerry's bunk.

"Everything went according to plan," he whispered. "Tomorrow you all start earning your ten per cent."

"Hold it," Phil said. "I thought I had already earned my ten per cent by getting Daniel to buy the rope for you."

"You haven't even started to earn it," Tom said. "Here is the way we will work it. Two of you will go with me to the washroom at seven thirty tomorrow night. One will have to stay and clean the washroom. The other one will go up to the attic with me to help with the rope. The third can remain in the dormitory. You will each take turns doing the different things that must be done to get the candy store going."

"Count me out," Phil said to Tom's surprise. "We will all get expelled for sure if we get caught smuggling candy into the academy."

Jerry shook his head. "What a worry wart you are," he said with disgust. "We haven't even opened the candy store and already you've got us all expelled."

"I can't help it," Phil said. "This is the only Catholic academy in Utah. And if I get expelled my mother and father will never forgive me."

Tom hadn't expected this. He looked at Tony.

"What about you, Tony?" he asked.

"Haw," Tony said.

"Cut out that haw business," Tom said. "Are you in or out?"

Tony hesitated a moment. "I think Phil is right," he said.

"In that case," Tom said, "would you and Phil mind leaving us? What I have to say is for the ears of stockholders in the corporation only. And Jerry and I will pick two other fellows to become stockholders."

Phil began biting his lip. "You mean we aren't friends anymore?" he asked.

Jerry spoke before Tom could answer. "Who wants to be friends with a couple of worry warts?" he asked.

"Jerry is right," Tom said. "We don't want to have anything to do with a couple of fellows who are going to be worrying all the time about something that can't happen."

"What do you mean it can't happen?" Phil demanded. "You can get caught smuggling candy into the academy and be expelled for it."

Tom tapped a finger to his temple. "When my great brain develops a plan," he said, "it is always foolproof. If I thought there was any chance of getting caught I would forget all about the candy store. I don't want to get expelled any more than you or Tony do. But since you are both so afraid it is better if you aren't stockholders. Now leave Jerry and me alone while we decide what two other kids we want for stockholders."

Phil and Tony got up and walked down to Phil's bunk.

Jerry looked at Tom. "What two other kids do you think we should get?" he asked.

"Phil and Tony will be back," Tom said confidently.

"Just pretend we are talking and looking over the other seventh graders."

Tom was right. Phil and Tony held a whispered conversation and then returned.

"We decided we wanted to be stockholders," Phil said.

"And your friends," Tony said. "I like you two better than any friends I've ever had."

"Welcome back to the corporation," Tom said.

Tom made his usual announcement the following night. Jerry and Tony went to the washroom. Tom entered it a couple of minutes later and locked the door from the inside. He showed Jerry the closet where the mops, rags, and cleaning things were kept. Then he and Tony climbed up to the attic. They tied knots in the rope at every two feet. Tom secured one end to a rafter and then let the rest of it down to the street.

Tony looked out the window. "Boy, that is a long way down," he said.

"Pull the rope up when I get to the sidewalk," Tom said. "Somebody might come along and see it. Drop it down when you see me coming back."

"If you ever get back," Tony said, shaking his head.

"Don't go soft on me now," Tom said.

He let himself down the rope hand-over-hand until his feet touched the sidewalk. He waited until Tony started pulling the rope up and then ran to the corner. He remembered seeing a neighborhood business district during his ride to the academy with Father O'Malley and Sweyn. He ran the five blocks to where it was located. A drugstore and a grocery store were still open. Tom tried the drugstore first because he knew the drugstore in Adenville carried candy. But this one had no candy. Then Tom entered the grocery store. This time he had better luck. The store carried a good stock of candy. A big fat man with muttonchop whiskers wearing a white apron was leaning on the counter. Tom ordered five peanut candy bars, five chocolate, five caramel, and five coconut. He handed the proprietor the last of his silver dollars.

"That is a lot of candy for just one boy," the man said.

"It isn't all for me," Tom said. "Are you open every night?"

"Until eight o'clock except on Sundays," the man answered.

"You will be seeing me once or twice a week," Tom said.

"Good," said the man. "I can use the business."

Tom had the candy put into a brown paper bag. He knew he had plenty of time so he walked back to the academy. Tony saw him coming and let down the rope. Tom rolled up the top of the paper bag and put it between his teeth. With the knots in the rope to assist him it was no trick at all to climb back up to the attic.

Jerry stared at the brown paper bag when Tom and Tony returned to the washroom. "You did it!" he exclaimed, forgetting to keep his voice down.

"Be quiet," Tom said.

"I'm all through except for mopping the floor," Jerry whispered.

With Jerry and Tony helping him, Tom got the floor mopped quickly. He made sure the coast was clear and let his two friends out of the washroom. He had to wait until the floor was dry. Then he put the bag of candy under

his shirt and went into the dormitory. His three friends were waiting for him on Jerry's bunk.

"The candy cost a dollar," he whispered. "If we sell all twenty bars at ten cents a bar the corporation will make a profit of one dollar. As ten-per-cent stockholders you will each receive a dime. As a seventy-per-cent stockholder I'll receive seventy cents."

"Before you start selling it," Jerry said, "how about each of us taking a bar of candy for ourselves?"

Tom's money-loving heart and great brain had anticipated this. He knew if they each took a bar of candy to eat, that would leave only sixteen bars of candy to sell, giving the corporation a profit of sixty cents. As ten-per-cent stockholders his three friends would be entitled to six cents each. This would leave him a profit of only fifty-two cents. And even if he sold his bar of candy for a dime his profit would only be sixty-two cents instead of seventy cents.

"We can't do that," he said, "unless I take seven bars of candy for each bar you take because I own seventy per cent of the corporation."

"The candy bars only cost a nickel," Jerry said. "Give us each a bar of candy and five cents for our share of the profits."

It was a good thing Tom had a great brain or he might have fallen for that one. I know I would have.

"If you eat a bar of candy," Tom said, "there is no profit on it. The only fair thing to do is for each of us to pay a dime for a bar of candy like everybody else."

Phil shook his head. "I forgot to ask my folks for money Sunday," he said.

"You don't need any money," Tom said. "Just take one bar of candy as your share of the profits."

Jerry nodded. "Let's do it that way," he said. "I'll take a bar of candy instead of my share of the profits."

"Me too," Tony said.

Tom removed the bag of candy from under his shirt. His three friends each took one bar. Tom took a chocolate bar for himself, which he put in his pocket.

"Now Phil," he said, "you go to the top of the stairway and act as lookout. If you see any of the priests coming up the stairs let me know."

Tom waited until Phil had left the dormitory. Then he dumped the sixteen bars of candy on his bunk and clapped his hands for attention.

"Step right up, fellows," he said. "The Academy Candy Store is now open for business. Get yourself a nice peanut, coconut, caramel, or chocolate bar for only a dime. No credit or promises. Cash only. Step right up, fellows. And remember to give me all the wrappers. You can't have the candy unless you give me the wrappers."

Tom knew it was important not to have any candy wrappers found by the priests. His plan was to put them in the paper bag and hide them under the statue of Saint Francis. Then on his next trip to the grocery store he would throw them away.

Tom had prepared the kids for this. Most of them had received money from their parents. He sold the sixteen bars of candy in about sixteen seconds. Poor old Sweyn didn't have any money and didn't get a bar of candy. He came over to Tom's bunk.

"I call that pretty darn selfish," he said. "All that

candy and you wouldn't give your own brother one bar of it."

"You could have got some money from home like the other kids did," Tom said. "And although I said no credit or promises that didn't include my own brother."

"It is too late now. It's all gone," Sweyn said as he looked with envy at all the kids chomping on candy bars.

Tom took the bar he had saved for himself and broke it in two. "You can have half of mine," he said, "but that is five cents you owe me."

Tom's money-loving heart and his great brain had a real battle for the next couple of days. His money-loving heart told him to make two trips to the grocery store each week. His great brain told him only to make one trip on Friday evenings. His great brain won the battle for two reasons. Every Friday evening from seven thirty to eight thirty Father Rodriguez and the other priests attended vespers in the chapel. It was the one hour during the week when Tom didn't have to worry about the superintendent coming to check on him in the washroom. And his great brain reminded him that if he brought too much candy into the academy some kid was liable to get a bellyache and have to go to the dispensary. And the boy might tell Father Rodriguez how he got the bellyache. Tom realized that he would have to be satisfied with a sixty-cent profit a week plus a bar of candy for himself.

All the boys including Tom were looking forward to their fourth Saturday at the academy. Father Rodriguez had announced they would go on a nature-study hike that would include a picnic. And he reminded students they would be permitted to purchase ten cents worth of candy. Tom knew he wouldn't sell any candy that week but it was worth it just knowing he would get outside the academy for one day.

Tom felt like a prisoner on parole as he marched out of the academy grounds on Saturday morning. Father Rodriguez led the boys with Father O'Malley and Father Petrie bringing up the rear, carrying a big basket of food. They marched to the business section five blocks from the academy to catch a streetcar.

They rode the streetcar to the end of the line and then hiked along a road until they came to a trail that led into a mountain canyon. They hiked two miles up the trail to a picnic ground. Tom admitted it was worth the walk just to see the aspen trees with their leaves so golden and orange at that time of year. And he enjoyed the nature-study lectures that Father Rodriguez gave because his great brain learned new things about plants and trees. They got to roast frankfurters over a campfire for lunch, which was a real treat.

Yes sir, Tom was really enjoying himself—until they returned to the city and got off the streetcar in the business district. It was time to buy the candy. And Tom knew the only place that sold candy in that neighborhood was the grocery store owned by the fat man. He tried to think of some way he could avoid entering the store. But Father Rodriguez put a stop to his wondering in a hurry.

"You boys will line up on the left and enter the store one at a time," the superintendent said. "I shall be inside to make certain you only buy ten cents worth of candy.

99

When you come out of the store, line up on the right side. Father O'Malley and Father Petrie will remain outside to make certain none of you tries to repeat."

It was like a sentence of death to the Academy Candy Store. Tom knew he would soon be expelled and on his way home. He leaned forward and whispered to Jerry.

"Better buy jawbreakers so they will last," he said. "This is the end of the Academy Candy Store. When the proprietor sees me it will be all over. He is bound to tell Father Rodriguez this is where I've been buying the candy."

I can't even describe the anguish Tom felt at that moment. Losing a profit of sixty cents a week plus a free bar of candy was enough to break any kid's heart, let alone a money-loving heart like Tom's. And believing he would be expelled was enough to make tears come into his eyes.

I know if I'd been in Tom's shoes at that moment, rather than return home in disgrace I would have run away and become a vagabond, a lost soul wandering from city to city and port to port for the rest of my days.

CHAPTER SEVEN

Goodness Doesn't Pay

TOM AND I HAD WORKED OUT a system before he went away to the academy. We both knew that Papa and Mamma would expect me to let them read any letters my brother wrote to me. To get around this, Tom always enclosed two letters in the envelope. One was a nice brotherly letter saying how much he missed me and the family. The other one gave me the real lowdown on what was happening at the academy. That was why I was astonished when the second monthly report arrived from Father Rodriguez. It was a good report saying Tom had gone an entire month without getting any demerits.

Papa was so flabbergasted that he read the report

twice. Even that didn't convince him his eyes weren't playing tricks on him. He had Mamma read the report aloud. And then, having convinced himself it was true, he immediately took all the credit.

"I told you it was just a matter of giving Tom time to adjust," he said proudly.

Papa hadn't told us any such thing. Mamma had been the one who said it. Papa often took credit for things Mamma said, but she usually let him get away with it.

The difference between the report and what Tom had written me about his second month at the academy left me with but one conclusion. The Great Brain was pulling the wool over the eyes of the Jesuit priests, just as he had done to a lot of adults in Adenville.

Now remember, when we left Tom he was standing in front of the grocery store where he had been buying candy for his candy store. He felt like a fellow about to enter the den of a hungry lion. He was sure the proprietor would tell on him and he would be expelled. Then he happened to look up at the sign over the store which read:

HAGEN'S GROCERY STORE
AND MEAT MARKET

This wouldn't mean a thing to a kid in Tom's shoes unless he had a great brain like my brother. Tom knew that Hagen was a German name and most Germans were Lutherans. His great brain told him that Mr. Hagen wasn't a Catholic, or else Father Rodriguez wouldn't have to stand guard to make sure no kid bought more than ten cents worth of candy. Also the owner of the store would be losing a dollar's worth of candy business a week if he told Father Rodriguez. Tom kept his fingers crossed as he entered the store. His future depended upon Mr. Hagen. The fat proprietor looked at him as if he had never seen him before and Tom uncrossed his fingers and smiled.

"What kind of candy do you want, young fellow?" Mr. Hagen asked.

Tom bought ten cents worth of licorice and peppermint sticks. He felt like whistling as he walked out of the store and joined Jerry in the line.

"He isn't going to tell," he whispered. "The candy store is still in business."

Tom wondered why Father Rodriguez was so strict about candy in the academy. He decided to ask Father O'Malley about it when school let out on Monday.

"Why does Father Rodriguez only let the fellows buy candy once every four weeks?" he asked.

"There was a time," Father O'Malley said, "when the boys could have all the sweets they wanted. Parents were permitted to bring candy every visiting day. Out-of-town parents were permitted to mail candy to their sons. And on Saturdays the boys could go to the store and buy all the candy they wanted."

"Why did Father Rodriguez stop it?" Tom asked.

"Because some of the boys ate so many sweets we had an epidemic of stomachaches," Father O'Malley answered. "And others weren't eating all of their meals to give them a balanced diet."

"That makes sense," Tom admitted. "But why doesn't Father Rodriguez tell that to the fellows instead of just saying candy is bad for the teeth and health?"

"It amounts to the same thing, doesn't it?" Father O'Malley answered.

103

Tom made a trip to the grocery store Friday evening while the priests were at vespers.

"I'll bet you have been wondering why I didn't tell on you," the fat proprietor said.

Tom knew the answer but wanted to hear what the man would say.

"Why didn't you tell?" he asked.

"I knew you had to be from the academy," Mr. Hagen said. "And I've heard those priests treat you kids like you were inmates in a reformatory. So I just kept my mouth shut."

Tom knew there was another reason. Mr. Hagen didn't want to lose a dollar's worth of candy business a week. But he didn't say anything.

As usual Jerry, Phil, and Tony each took a bar of candy as their share of the profits. Tom kept a bar for himself and sold the rest, making a neat profit of sixty cents. Everything was just hunky-dory until the next morning when Father Rodriguez sent for Tom. The Great Brain couldn't imagine what the superintendent wanted, unless some kid had snitched about the candy store. He was expecting the usual stern look on the priest's face when he entered the superintendent's office. Instead, for the first time, he saw Father Rodriguez actually smiling.

"I know you have anxiously been waiting for this day to arrive," Father Rodriguez said.

"I have, Father?" Tom asked, puzzled. "Why?"

"Come now, Thomas," the priest chided him. "I know you have been counting the days you have been cleaning the washroom. And as of today you have gone an entire month without getting a single demerit. I congratulate you."

Tom sure as heck didn't feel like being congratulated. He felt like giving himself a hard kick in the behind for not remembering to get some demerits so he wouldn't lose the washroom job. Without it the Academy Candy Store would be out of business. He had to keep that job.

"I would hate to have it on my conscience," he said, " that some boy failed because he didn't have enough time to study on account of having to clean the washroom. Losing part of my study period doesn't bother me because of my great brain. So maybe you should make the washroom my permanent work assignment."

"You are really full of surprises today," the priest said. "The boy who cleans the washroom has ample time to study. Your permanent work assignment will be the hallway on the dormitory floor. You will sweep and dust it every day and on Saturdays you will mop and polish it."

Tom made one desperate last attempt to save his candy store. "If you haven't anybody to do the job," he said, "I can take care of the washroom until you get somebody."

"Boys being boys," Father Rodriguez said, "I never run out of boys to peel potatoes and clean the washroom. John Burton will clean it for one week starting today for throwing spitballs in the classroom. He will be followed by William Daniels for two weeks for coming late to class. And by that time others will be waiting. You are excused, Thomas."

Tom felt so far down in the dumps as he left the superintendent's office that it would have taken a team of mules to pull him out. He knew his money-loving heart would never forgive his great brain for losing him a profit of sixty cents a week. All he had to do was to get just five demerits a month and he could have kept the washroom job until school ended.

He went into the yard where his three friends were waiting for him under their usual tree. He told them what had happened.

"I guess my great brain went to sleep on me," he concluded. "We sure as heck can't make every kid who gets the washroom job a stockholder in the corporation."

Jerry shook his head sadly. "Good-bye, candy store," he said. "The washroom is the only way to get into the attic."

That made Tom's great brain wake up in a hurry. "Wrong," he said. "What about the storeroom on the third floor? I bet there's a trapdoor into the attic from it."

"So what?" Jerry asked. "The door is always locked. And Father Rodriguez carries the keys on that ring and chain he always has with him."

"Maybe not," Tom said. "Remember the ring of keys hanging on the wall in his office? I'll bet they are a duplicate set in case one of the priests needs them when Father Rodriguez isn't here. There is only one way to find out."

His three friends looked at him as if he was suggesting they steal the crucifix from the altar in the chapel. Phil was the first to recover from his astonishment.

"You get caught in his office when he isn't there and you'll be expelled for sure," he said.

"I'll put my great brain to work on it," Tom said, "and I personally guarantee we won't be caught."

I guess Tom's great brain wanted to redeem itself for not reminding him to get some demerits, because he had a plan all ready by the following Friday. He met with his three friends in the yard after school. He rehearsed them on what each had to do while the priests were at vespers that evening.

At seven thirty-five Tom and his three friends left the dormitory. Phil remained at the foot of the stairway on the ground floor. Tony went into the library. Tom and Jerry walked over to the doorway of the superintendent's office. Jerry had a textbook with him and they pretended to be arguing about a problem in it. They had to wait a couple of minutes before Phil signaled that no kids were coming down the stairway and Tony signaled that no kids were leaving the library. Then Tom opened the door of the office and slipped inside. He got the ring of keys and put them in his pocket. He scratched on the door and waited until he heard Jerry scratch back. Then he stepped out into the hallway, closing the door behind him.

He and Jerry went up the stairs to the third floor, with Tony and Phil following them. Phil went inside the dormitory. Tony stood at the top of the stairway. Tom and Jerry went to the door of the storeroom.

"We are all set," Tom whispered. "Phil will stop any kid coming out of the dormitory. Tony will let us know if anybody is coming up the stairway. John Burton has the door of the washroom locked so he can clean it. I'll start trying the keys now."

Tom tried four keys before he found the one that opened the storeroom. Inside there was enough moonlight coming through the windows for them to see more religious statues, crates, and boxes. But Tom was only interested in

the ceiling. And in one corner of it he saw a trapdoor lead-
ing to the attic. They slipped out and locked the door.

Then Tom and Jerry went down to the washroom on
the second floor and Tom made an impression of the key
in a bar of soap. He wiped the key off carefully before going back to the third floor and hiding the bar of soap under the statue of Saint Francis. Jerry got Phil from the dormitory and the four of them returned to the ground floor,
where they took up the same positions as before. When
the coast was clear Tom slipped into the superintendent's
office and returned the ring of keys to the peg on the wall.

Everything had been so easy up to this point that
Tom expected to hear Jerry scratching on the door immediately. Instead a minute passed, and then another minute, and Tom began to sweat. It seemed like an hour but
was actually only about five minutes before Jerry finally
scratched on the door. Tom slipped into the hallway.

"What took you so long?" Tom asked.

"Two eighth graders were standing in the doorway of
the library talking," Jerry said. "I couldn't just stand here
without attracting suspicion so I went into the library until they left."

Tom met with his three friends at their usual tree in
the yard the next afternoon. He had a piece of wood, the
bar of soap, and his pocketknife. He sat on the far side of
the tree so his three friends could warn him if anybody ap-
proached. Tom was an expert whittler and could carve just
about anything. But it took him more than an hour to
make a wooden key from the impression in the bar of
soap. He hid the key under the statue of Saint Francis.

That night he lay awake until all the other boys were

asleep. He got a black crayon and his pocketknife and crept into the hallway. He removed the wooden key from under the statue and tried it in the lock of the storeroom door. It didn't work. He then rubbed the black crayon on the key and tried it again. He went into the washroom and turned on the lights. He could tell from the crayon marks that the key had to be carved in two places. He did the carving and once again tried the key in the storeroom lock. It turned halfway and stopped. Again he rubbed the black crayon on it and tried again. He went into the washroom. The crayon marks told him that he had to make the notch on top deeper. He did this and once again tried the key. This time the wooden key opened the lock. Thanks to Tom's great brain the Academy Candy Store was back in business.

All the fellows had complained so much about the candy store's being closed the week before that Tom decided to buy forty five-cent bars of candy instead of twenty the following Friday evening. Of course, his money-loving heart had something to do with the decision because he had lost sixty cents in profit the week before. He waited until Billy Daniels went to clean the washroom and the priests were at vespers in the chapel. He left Phil in the dormitory to warn if anybody was coming out. There was nobody in the hallway. Jerry went down to the library where he could watch the clock. Tom and Tony entered the storeroom and locked the door behind them. They climbed on top of crates and entered the attic through the trapdoor. Tony remained in the attic while Tom made the trip to the grocery store and back. He had forty bars of candy in the paper sack.

Jerry was supposed to wait twenty minutes in the library and then return to the third floor. But when Tom scratched on the door there was no answering scratch from Jerry. Tom waited a couple of minutes and then scratched again. He heard Jerry scratch on the door and unlocked it. With Jerry shielding him from anybody coming up the stairway Tom locked the door and hid the key under the statue of Saint Francis.

The candy-hungry boys sure made up for the week the candy store had been closed. Tom made a profit of a dollar and twenty cents besides two bars of candy for himself and each of his three friends. And that night he got his first good night's sleep since losing his job in the washroom. I guess his money-loving heart had been keeping him awake.

CHAPTER EIGHT

The Mental Marvel

TOM HAD NEVER LIKED liver and wouldn't eat it on a bet. When he wrote me that they served beef liver every Thursday at the academy I sure felt sorry for him. Mamma said all boys disliked some kind of food. Tom hated liver. Sweyn wouldn't eat a tomato, raw or cooked. I hated celery; for my money, it was food for rabbits and not for human beings. Papa never ate radishes because they gave him gas. Mamma made gooseberry pies for us but never ate a piece herself. So what Mamma should have said is that all adults as well as all boys disliked some kind of food.

Tom wrote me that he tried to fill up on bread and

saved his candy bar to eat on Thursday nights. But this wasn't enough to stop him from going to bed hungry. Then one Thursday evening his great brain told him it was stupid to go to bed hungry when there was plenty to eat in the kitchen. He called Jerry, Phil, and Tony over to his bunk.

"How would you fellows like to have a nice sandwich tonight?" he asked.

Phil rubbed his stomach. "I could go for a jam sandwich," he said.

"Me too," Tony said.

Jerry nodded. "I guess we all could. But how are we going to get them?"

"We wait until the priests have gone to bed," Tom said, "and then sneak down to the kitchen."

"It is too risky," Phil said. "One of the priests might come into the kitchen to get a glass of milk or something."

"And besides," Tony said, "that would be stealing."

"No it wouldn't," Tom said. "Our parents are paying for our room and board. The food in the kitchen is there to feed us. So how can you call it stealing when we are just taking something that belongs to us?"

Phil shrugged. "All right," he said, "maybe it isn't stealing but it is too risky. We might even be expelled if we are caught."

Jerry looked disgusted. "There goes the worry wart again," he said. "We haven't even entered the kitchen and he has already got us all expelled."

"I wish you would stop calling me a worry wart," Phil said.

"I will stop when you stop acting like one," Jerry said.

113

"No sense in arguing," Tom said. "You and I will raid the kitchen, Jerry. And if Phil and Tony are afraid we'll bring them back a sandwich."

Tom guessed right what Jerry would say.

"If they want a sandwich let them come with us," he said.

"I'm not afraid," Tony said.

"Me neither," said Phil.

"All right," Tom said. "Just stay awake until the other fellows are asleep."

Tom lay awake, his stomach growling from hunger, until he was sure everybody but his three friends were asleep. But Jerry was the only one who wasn't asleep. They had to wake up Phil and Tony. They put on their slippers and slid down the banister to the ground floor. There was enough moonlight coming through the kitchen windows for them to see. Tom found a loaf of bread and sliced it. Then he got a piece of leftover baked ham from the icebox. Tom made himself a ham sandwich while his three friends made jam sandwiches. When they finished eating, Tom was still hungry and made himself a jam sandwich.

"Let's all have another one," Jerry said. "And how about a glass of milk?"

"Why not?" Tom asked.

Jerry patted his stomach after they had finished. "This is the best idea your great brain ever had," he said. "We can come down here every night and have a feast."

"No we can't," Tom said. "Father Petrie would get suspicious. We will only come on Thursday nights. You fellows know that is the night we have liver and I can't eat it."

The following Thursday night Tom and his three friends again raided the kitchen. Again Jerry said it was the best idea Tom's great brain ever had. But he was singing a different tune one week later. The four of them were sitting in the kitchen eating jam sandwiches and drinking milk when the kitchen lights went on. Standing in the doorway were Father Rodriguez and Father Petrie. Although Tom and his friends had on white nightgowns, they sure didn't look like four little angels. Angels don't have jam on their mouths and guilty looks on their faces.

"Finish your sandwiches and milk, boys," Father Rodriguez said, looking like a cat that has just cornered four mice. "You will all report to me in my office immediately after school tomorrow." Then he turned and walked out of the kitchen.

Tom stared at Father Petrie. "How did you know?" he asked.

"Bless my soul, Thomas," the fat priest said. "A cook knows what is in his kitchen just as a boy knows what is in his pockets. I missed the bread, jam, and milk taken the last two Thursday nights."

Tom and his three friends finished their sandwiches and milk but without much appetite. As they started up the stairway to the dormitory Phil turned to Tom.

"You and your great brain sure got us into a mess this time," he said. "I just knew we would get caught."

"If you knew," Jerry said, "why did you come with us?"

"Because I would rather get caught," Phil said, "than have you and Tom think I was afraid."

"Me too," Tony said.

115

"Don't worry, fellows," Tom said. "I'll take all the blame."

Phil grunted in disgust. "You took all the blame last time," he said, "but Jerry, Tony, and I ended up peeling spuds for three weeks."

The next day Tom felt a little hurt because Phil and Tony seemed to be avoiding him. A few minutes after three o'clock that afternoon they all stood before Father Rodriguez in the superintendent's office.

The priest rubbed his forehead as if very tired. "Thomas Fitzgerald," he said, "you are yet going to make me wish I had been born a Protestant."

"I take all the blame," Tom said.

"You usually do," the superintendent said. "But the four of you raided the kitchen and the four of you will be punished for it. Making you peel potatoes or clean the washroom seems to have no effect upon your deportment. But I do have a punishment in mind that may make you wish you had never raided the kitchen."

Tom couldn't think of any punishment worse than peeling spuds or cleaning the washroom. "What is that?" he asked.

"Twice each school year," Father Rodriguez said, "I permit all the students to attend the Salt Lake Theater. Our first trip to the theater is this coming Saturday afternoon. But now you four boys aren't going to be permitted to go."

"Please don't do that," Tom pleaded. "I've never been inside a theater. Make us peel potatoes, clean the washroom, give us demerits, anything you want, but please, Father, let us go to the theater."

116

"The punishment stands," Father Rodriguez said. "You boys are excused."

"It isn't fair," Tom cried, "to give us such a severe punishment just because I can't eat liver."

Father Rodriguez leaned forward on his desk. "What has liver to do with your raiding the kitchen?" he asked.

"I can't eat any kind of liver," Tom said. "I hate the sight, smell, and taste of it. And I got so hungry on Thursday nights that I talked the fellows into raiding the kitchen with me."

"Do you mean to tell me that the only reason you raided the kitchen was because you were hungry?" Father Rodriguez asked.

"Yes, Father," Tom answered.

"Why didn't you tell me that you didn't like liver?" the superintendent asked.

"What good would it do?" Tom asked. "There is no prayer you could say for me that would make me eat liver."

"I never want any boy in this academy to go to bed hungry," Father Rodriguez said. "I shall arrange with Father Petrie to give you fried eggs on Thursdays for supper, Thomas. And I don't think I can punish you, because I've been remiss in my duties as a superintendent and priest. I should have made certain all the boys were eating the food served them at every meal."

"Does that mean we can go to the theater Saturday?" Tom asked.

"Yes," Father Rodriguez said. "There will be no punishment for any of you. You are excused."

"Thank you, Father," Tom said. "Thank you very much."

Tom's three friends patted him on the back after they were out of the superintendent's office.

"Your great brain did it again," Jerry said. "You talked Father Rodriguez right out of punishing us."

"It wasn't my great brain at all," Tom said. It was the first time he hadn't given his great brain all the credit. "I simply told the truth."

Jerry grinned. "Then just go on telling the truth and maybe that will make a Protestant out of Father Rodriguez," he said. "That would be one way to get rid of him."

"Yeah," Phil said, "especially since it looks as if the Pope isn't going to answer your letter."

Tom couldn't help feeling that maybe Father Rodriguez wasn't such a bad fellow after all. "Just what makes you think another superintendent would be any better?" he asked.

"Anybody," Jerry said, "would be better than Father Rodriguez."

"I am beginning to wonder after what just happened," Tom said. "It is like my father used to say when we went on a fishing and camping trip and the road was bad. There is always a worse road than the one you are traveling on."

Tom was just as excited as the rest of the boys when they entered the Salt Lake Theater for the Saturday matinee accompanied by Father Rodriguez and Father O'Malley.

The theater was famous for the plays, operas, concerts, and vaudeville shows held there. Father Rodriguez had chosen a week when a vaudeville show was playing. Tom was thrilled with the theater itself and with the show.

There were acrobats, a trained-seal act, a song-and-dance team, a comedian, a quartet, some Swiss bell ringers, and, as the headliner, a mind-reading act called the Mental Marvel.

It was this act all the fellows liked best. The Mental Marvel had two people from the audience come up on the stage and blindfold him. Then his assistant mingled with the audience, asking people to hand him some article they had on their person. The assistant would hold the article in his hand and ask the Mental Marvel to read his mind and tell the audience what it was. And just like a shot the Mental Marvel would say it was a watch, a billfold, a pair of glasses, or whatever the article happened to be.

Tom was as mystified as the other boys until he put his great brain to work. He was positive that no one could read another person's mind. There had to be some trick to it. He watched and listened very carefully to every word the assistant said.

The fellows were talking about the Mental Marvel all the way back to the dormitory.

"The Mental Marvel's brain makes your great brain look about the size of a pea," Rory Flynn said to Tom. "Just imagine being able to read other people's minds."

"If the Mental Marvel could really read minds," Tom said, "he wouldn't be traveling around the country in a vaudeville show. He could be making a fortune."

"How?" Rory asked.

"Many ways," Tom said. "He could become a gambler and know what cards the other players are holding."

"Not if he is an honest man," Rory said. "You are just jealous because you can't read minds like the Mental Marvel."

"Jerry and I could do the same thing with a little practice," Tom said.

"Talk is cheap," Rory said. "I'll bet you can't."

Tom was pretty confident he knew how it was done. But he wanted to make sure before he put up any hard cash. And he knew if he acted reluctant that would make Rory and the other kids all the more eager to bet. His great brain and money-loving heart were working like sixty to turn this to his financial advantage.

"Just have your money ready after supper on Monday night," Tom said.

Tom walked over to his bunk and sat down with his three friends.

"Boy, oh, boy," Jerry said. "You sure stuck your neck out that time. You know you can't read my mind, even with your great brain."

"Nobody can read another person's mind," Tom said. "But my great brain did figure out how the Mental Marvel and his assistant put on their mind-reading act. I just need to work out the details. Phil will be visiting his folks tomorrow so you and Tony meet me in our usual spot in the yard. I'll have it all figured out by then."

When Tom met Jerry and Tony under their usual tree the next afternoon he had a notebook with him.

"First," he said, "let me explain how the Mental Marvel knew what the assistant held in his hand. I noticed that each time, the assistant asked a slightly different question. They used a code word for each article. For example, when the assistant said, 'Please read my mind, Mental Marvel, and tell me what I hold in my hand,' the code word 'please' meant it was a watch. My great brain has figured out dif-

120

ferent words I can begin a sentence with. All you've got to do, Jerry, is to memorize those words and the articles they are code words for. I made up two lists, one for each of us."

He tore a sheet from the notebook and handed it to Jerry. On it he had printed the following:

CAN means it is a CATECHISM
TELL means it is a ROSARY
OH means it is HOLY MEDALS
THIS means it is a PAIR OF GLASSES
WHAT means it is a RING
YOU means it is a WATCH
SEARCH means it is MONEY
READ means it is a LETTER
IF means it is a POCKETKNIFE
IT means it is a CRUCIFIX
I means it is a PENCIL
WILL means it is a COMB

Jerry looked at the list. "What if it is something we don't have a code word for?" he asked.

"We've got a code word for just about everything the fellows would have on them at the theater," Tom said. "But if one of them does hold out something we don't have a code word for I'll do the same thing the assistant did and just pass them by. Start memorizing the code words now. And after supper go to the chapel where it is nice and quiet and do some more memorizing instead of praying. We will meet here tomorrow after school for a rehearsal."

Tom knew he could memorize the code words in no time. He had picked Jerry to be his partner because the red-headed boy had a better memory than Phil or Tony. The four of them met in the yard on Monday after school. Tom tested Jerry until he was satisfied Jerry knew all the code words. Then he and Jerry began rehearsing sentences beginning with code words. By the time they returned to the dormitory to wash up for supper Tom knew that both he and Jerry had the parts they would play down pat.

After supper Tom waited until the four kids assigned to the kitchen and dining room were finished before he began the demonstration. His money-loving heart didn't want to miss any bets. He had put the paper bag containing the profits from the candy store under his pillow. He was now ready to lead the lamb to the slaughter. He removed the bag.

"Do you still want to bet, Rory, that Jerry and I can't do what the Mental Marvel and his assistant did?" he asked.

"Sure," Rory said. "But you must do it exactly like they did it."

"I will let you blindfold Jerry and place him at one end of the dormitory," Tom said. "And to make it even tougher you can make him face the wall. I will stand at the other end of the dormitory. You fellows will hand me articles you had with you at the theater. I will ask Jerry to identify them. If he misses one article I lose the bet. Now, how many of you fellows want to bet besides Rory?"

Those kids must have thought they had a sure thing. Every one of them except Tom's three friends raised their hands.

"Phil," Tom said, "you go to the top of the stairway

and act as lookout. Tony, get a notebook and write down the name of each fellow and how much he bets."

Tom then dumped his profits from the candy store onto his bunk. "Get in line now to bet," he said. "You tell Tony how much you want to put down. He'll write your name and the amount and hand the money to me. I'll drop it in the paper bag and then cover each bet with my own money. After all bets are made, my brother Sweyn will hold the stakes. If you fellows win, he can take the notebook and pay each of you double the amount you bet from the paper bag. Any questions?"

The boys lined up like sheep waiting to be sheared by The Great Brain. Rory was first in line.

"I wish I had more than forty cents to bet," he said.

"So do I," Tom said. "So do I."

Sweyn was next and bet fifty cents. "This is one time your great brain and big mouth are going to cost you plenty," he said. "A joke is a joke but you can still call it off."

"If you are so sure it can't be done," Tom said, "why don't you bet a dollar?"

"Because fifty cents is all I've got," Sweyn said.

By the time all bets had been placed, there was more than ten dollars in the paper bag. Tom stood to make a fortune if he or Jerry didn't make a mistake. And he stood to lose a fortune if they did. If that happened his money-loving heart would break wide open.

"All right, Rory," he said. "Take Jerry to the end of the dormitory, blindfold him, and face him against the wall. The rest of you get ready to hand me articles you had on you at the theater."

"Wait for me," Rory said. "I want to be first because I know that will be the end of the demonstration."

A few minutes later the mind-reading demonstration was ready to begin. Rory handed Tom his rosary.

"Tell me, Mental Marvel, what I am holding in my hand," Tom said.

"A rosary," Jerry answered.

There was a gasp of astonishment from all the fellows except Sweyn. "It was just a lucky guess," he said, holding out his watch.

Tom took it. "You will have to read my mind, Mental Marvel, to tell me what this is," he said.

"A watch," Jerry answered.

Larry Williams handed Tom his pocket-sized catechism.

"Can you read my mind, Mental Marvel, and tell me what this article is?" Tom asked.

"A catechism," Jerry answered.

By this time the fellows who had bet were staring at Tom as if he was the devil himself. He took a letter from the next student.

"Read my mind, Mental Marvel, and tell me what I hold in my hand," he said.

"A letter," Jerry answered.

Billy Daniels removed a ring from his finger and handed it to Tom.

"What am I holding in my hand now, Mental Marvel?" Tom asked.

"A ring," Jerry answered.

Willie Connors handed Tom his pocketknife.

"If you can tell me what I hold in my hand now," Tom said, "you are truly a Mental Marvel."

124

"A pocketknife," Jerry answered.

Tom returned the pocketknife. "That ends the demonstration," he said. "Jerry and I have proved how the Mental Marvel and his assistant did their mind-reading act, and I've won all bets."

Harold Adams took off his glasses and held them out. "Just one more, please," he said.

Tom took the glasses. "This is the last time you have to read my mind, Mental Marvel, and tell what I hold in my hand," he said.

"A pair of glasses," Jerry answered.

Tom gave the glasses back. "That ends the demonstration for sure," he said. In his letter he wrote me that he had never seen such a bunch of open-mouthed kids. They couldn't have been more astonished if he and Jerry had jumped out the window and started flying around like birds.

He told Jerry to take off the blindfold and then got the paper bag with the money in it from Sweyn.

"I figured Rory and the others would bet," he said, "but I didn't think my own brother would be that foolish."

Poor Sweyn was still in a daze, not only from what he'd seen and heard but also from losing half a dollar. "I still don't believe it," he said. "How did you do it?"

Rory nodded his head. "You have won our money," he said, "and that entitles us to know how it was done."

"I don't remember promising I would tell you how it was done," Tom said. His money-loving heart told him to make them pay to find out. But his great brain reminded him that this was a good time to get even with the eighth graders for the torture tunnel. And anyway he had won all their money.

"The only way you are ever going to find out how it was done," he said, "is for the eighth graders to go through the torture tunnel of the seventh graders."

Rory folded his arms on his chest. "I'm not going to let you little seventh graders paddle me," he said.

Sweyn grabbed Rory's arm. "Yes you are," he said. "It is worth it to find out how it was done."

Larry Williams nodded his head. "Sweyn is right," he said. "And if you don't want all the eighth graders giving you the silent treatment you'll do as Tom says."

Rory knew he was beat as all the other eighth graders began nodding their heads. "All right," he said. "You little seventh graders get your torture tunnel ready."

Tom got the seventh graders lined up in the aisle with their legs apart and their geography books in their hands.

"Give it to them good and hard like they gave it to us," he ordered.

After the last eighth graders had crawled through the torture tunnel all the kids gathered around Tom. He explained how the Mental Marvel and his assistant worked with code words and then showed them the sheet of paper with the words he and Jerry had used.

Sweyn pointed at the sheet. "What if somebody held up an article you and Jerry didn't have a code word for?" he asked.

"I'd do the same thing the assistant did in the theater," Tom said, "and just pass them up."

Sweyn nodded. "You're right," he said. "I noticed how the assistant passed up a lot of people. Why, he even ignored Rory, who was right near him holding out his rosary."

"That is because they didn't have a code word for a

rosary," Tom said. "No more questions, please. To figure this all out put a strain on my great brain and I want to give it a rest."

Tom didn't really want to give his great brain a rest. All he wanted to do was count the money and find out how much he had won.

"Anybody could have figured it out," Rory said.

"Then why didn't you figure it out and save yourself forty cents and a paddling?" Tom asked with a grin.

"You've got a smart mouth," Rory said. "And one of these days I'm going to close it for you."

Tom handed the paper bag to Jerry. "I'll back up anything I say with my fists any time," he said.

Sweyn stepped between them. "You start a fight in the dormitory and you'll both be expelled," he said.

Tom had believed from his first day at the academy that he would have to fight Rory sooner or later. His great brain had planned how to do it without being expelled.

"Who is going to know there has been a fight?" he asked. "Rory and I will go into the washroom, where nobody can see us. And after I give him a black eye and a bloody nose he can tell Father Rodriguez he fell down the stairs."

"He is bigger and older than you," Sweyn said.

"So what," Tom said. "You know that with my correspondence course in boxing from John L. Sullivan and all my experience fighting in Adenville, I've whipped kids a lot bigger and tougher than him." Then he looked at Rory. "You've been digging at me since school started. Let's go to the washroom and settle it right now."

Now I'm not saying that Rory Flynn was a coward. But after hearing Tom confidently say he would black

128

Rory's eye and bloody his nose, and then hearing about that course in boxing from the former champion of the world and about Tom's whipping kids bigger and tougher, for my money Rory would have been a fool to fight Tom.

"I'm not going to get expelled on account of you," Rory said. He walked to his bunk and sat down.

Jerry patted Tom on the back. "You sure bluffed him," he said.

"I wasn't bluffing," Tom said. "Rory is just a big bag of wind."

But Tom was going to learn that a big bag of wind can blow a fellow right into a lot of trouble, as he told me in his next letter.

CHAPTER NINE

Mystery of the Missing Mattress

PAPA HAD HIS ANNUAL physical checkup with
Dr. LeRoy just two days before the November reports on
Tom and Sweyn arrived from the academy. It was a good
thing Dr. LeRoy pronounced Papa in excellent health. I
say this because Papa would have had a nervous breakdown and apoplexy all at once after reading the report on
Tom. The report informed us that Tom had received fifteen demerits for the month, just five short of being expelled. The news made Papa do something I'd never seen
him do before. He always took a drink of brandy before
supper but that was all he ever drank. But after reading
the report he went into the pantry and poured himself a

130

big glass of brandy. He drank it and then returned to the parlor, where he began pacing up and down like a caged animal.

"I knew it couldn't last," he cried out. "Mark my words, Tom will be expelled before Christmas."

This was certainly a switch from the month before when he said he knew Tom just needed a little time to adjust. But Papa was like that. He took credit when it was a credit to do so and neatly shifted the blame when it wasn't.

That was one time I wanted to confess that Tom had been enclosing two letters in his envelopes. I wanted to tell Papa that it wasn't Tom's fault, because my brother had written me all about it. But I knew if I showed Papa that one letter he would insist on reading all the letters Tom had sent me. And that would have given him a nervous breakdown and apoplexy even if he was in perfect health.

It was all Rory Flynn's fault that Tom had got fifteen demerits. It began one morning when Tom returned to the dormitory after breakfast and found a blue slip on his bunk. A blue slip meant an infraction of a rule and whoever received one had to report to the superintendent's office after classes. One of the rules of the academy was that all bunks had to be made up before the boys went to breakfast. Then, after saying Grace Before Meals, Father Rodriguez would go to the dormitory for an inspection while the fellows were eating. Tom knew darn well that he had made up his bunk. Now it was all mussed up. And he was pretty sure Rory had done it. But there wasn't anything he could do but report to the superintendent's office. He was given five demerits.

Another rule was that all students had to have all

their textbooks when reporting for class in the morning. The reason for this was that some of the students used to leave textbooks which they'd been using for homework in the dormitory. This meant Father O'Malley had to hold up the class until the students went and got their books.

Two days after Tom had received five demerits for not making up his bunk he couldn't find his textbook on advanced arithmetic after breakfast. He was positive he had left it on his desk with the other textbooks. He looked all around but couldn't find it. He knew he couldn't bluff it in class so he told Father O'Malley he had lost his advanced arithmetic textbook. He was sent to the superintendent's office and received another five demerits. Kenneth Bradley, whose permanent work assignment was to sweep and dust the library after school, found Tom's textbook lying on a table in the library. Tom knew he hadn't been to the library the night before. And he was now positive that Rory Flynn was behind all this.

The following week Tom found another blue slip on his bunk for not making up his bed.

"This makes fifteen demerits this month," Father Rodriguez said as he pronounced sentence in his office after school that day. "Why have you suddenly become so careless and lazy?"

Tom knew he was neither careless nor lazy. He also knew he couldn't tell the superintendent what he believed to be true without being a tattletale.

"It won't happen again, Father," he said.

"It had better not," the priest said. "You are excused."

Tom joined his three friends under the tree in the yard.

"We all know Rory is doing this to get even with me

for making him back down when I wanted to fight him," Tom said. "I saw he was the last one in the dining room for breakfast this morning. He just waited until everybody was out of the dormitory and then mussed up my bunk like he did before."

Jerry scratched his head. "How did he plant the textbook in the library?" he asked.

"He waited until everybody had left the dormitory that morning," Tom said. "Then he took the textbook and hid it. And he probably sneaked it into the library during the noon hour. If I get five more demerits I can be expelled. We've got to stop Rory."

"I've got it," Jerry said. "Let's wait until he goes to sleep tonight and then take all his clothes and soak them in water and tie them in knots. That will get him demerits for showing up late for breakfast."

Tom shook his head. "He would only do the same to me while I'm asleep," he said.

"How about putting rocks under his mattress?" Phil asked, picking up a rock.

"He would just put rocks under my mattress," Tom said. "But you have given me an idea, Phil. I'll put my great brain to work on it."

Tom's great brain had a plan all figured out by Saturday. He had to take the entire seventh grade into his confidence to make it work. This didn't worry him because he knew none of the kids liked Rory and class spirit would make them cooperate. He marched down to the dimly lit chapel with his classmates for confession. They sat down on their side of the chapel and the eighth graders sat on the opposite side.

"Now remember," Tom whispered, "you go first,

133

Jerry, and make it the shortest confession on record. Then you go, Tony, and make it the longest confession on record. If I'm not back by the time you come out of the confessional Phil will go and make his confession a good long one."

The tinkle of a bell in the seventh-grade confessional was heard. Jerry got up and walked toward it just as the tinkle of a bell was heard on the eighth-grade side. Tom watched an eighth grader start for the confessional and then dropped down on his hands and knees. He crawled along the aisle on the seventh-grade side to the rear of the chapel and from there into the hallway.

Everything now depended upon split-second timing. Tom ran up to the third floor. He got the key from under the statue of Saint Francis and unlocked the storeroom door. Then he went to the dormitory and removed the bed clothing from Rory's bunk. He carried Rory's mattress into the storeroom, locked the door, and returned the wooden key to its hiding place. Then he went back to the dormitory and made up Rory's bunk without a mattress. From there he crept down the stairway.

Jerry was in the hallway and motioned to him that the coast was clear. Tom ran to the chapel, crawled on his hands and knees down the seventh-grade side, and took his place beside Phil before Tony came out of the confessional.

Tom didn't receive any heavy penance from Father O'Malley this time, because he could honestly say he hadn't broken the fourth commandment and that he didn't dislike Father Rodriguez anymore. He came out of the chapel with Larry Williams and told him he was going to the library.

134

Tom and his three friends had been sitting in the library for about fifteen minutes when Willie Connors came running into the room.

"Somebody stole Rory's mattress," he said. "You had better get up to the dorm, Tom, before he takes yours."

Tom and his three friends and half a dozen other kids ran up to the dormitory. They arrived just as Rory was pulling the covers from Tom's bunk.

"Just what do you think you are doing?" Tom asked.

"I know you fellows took my mattress," Rory said, "so I'm going to take yours until you give me mine back."

"No you won't," said Tom.

"You bet you won't," Jerry said.

"Better not try it," added Phil.

Sweyn had come from the chapel and was listening. "Why would anybody want your mattress when they've got one of their own?" he asked. "Are you sure it is gone, Rory?"

"Look for yourself," Rory said.

Tom walked over to Rory's bunk with Sweyn and his three friends.

"It is gone," Tom said, looking as surprised as a dog who finds its buried bone is missing.

"It sure is," Jerry said.

Phil shook his head as if bewildered. "Why would anybody want to take Rory's mattress?" he asked.

"That is a good question," Tom said, "because it gives us the answer. *Nobody* would want to take Rory's mattress, which means he must have got rid of it himself."

Sweyn stared at Tom with a dumb look on his face. "Why would he want to get rid of his own mattress?" he asked.

136

"I don't like to say what I think happened in front of all you fellows," Tom said.

"Go ahead and say it!" Rory shouted.

"Well," Tom said, "I think you wet the bed last night and didn't want any of the fellows to see the stain. You were so ashamed, you knew you had to get rid of the mattress. And you remembered the old junkman who passes by every Saturday night. So you threw the mattress out the window, knowing the junkman would pick it up."

Rory looked as if he were going to explode. "I didn't wet the bed!" he shouted. "I haven't wet the bed since I was a baby! And I didn't throw my mattress out the window!"

"All right," Tom said with a straight face. "No sense in getting all riled up about it. Some of your eighth-grade friends are probably playing a joke on you. Did you look in the washroom?"

"That is the first place I looked," Rory said.

"Did you look in the classrooms and washroom on the second floor?" Tom asked.

"I looked there too," Rory said.

Tom shook his head. "I'm sure nobody would carry your mattress all the way down to the ground floor to hide it," he said. "That leaves only one conclusion."

"What conclusion?" Rory demanded.

"That I was right in the first place," Tom said. "Maybe it isn't too late." He walked over and looked down into the street. "Too late," he said. "The junkman has already picked it up."

Rory doubled up his fists. "I didn't wet the bed and I didn't throw my mattress out the window!" he shouted. "I know you took it and I'm going to make you tell me where you put it. I would rather be expelled for fighting than let the fellows think I wet the bed."

Tom spread out his hands. "How do you like that, fellows?" he said. "Rory wants to fight me because he wet the bed. I sure as heck didn't make him wet the bed."

All the kids began to laugh except Rory. Then Tom's face became serious.

"I'll fight you now or any time you want," he said. "And you might as well get expelled for fighting because when Father Rodriguez finds out you wet the bed and threw your mattress out the window for the junkman he will expel you anyway."

Sweyn stepped between them. He knew The Great Brain better than Rory and the other kids. "This has gone far enough," he said. "All right, T.D., where is the mattress? All Rory has to do is to tell Father Rodriguez that you took it and you'll be the one who is expelled."

Tom looked as innocent as a newborn baby. "That is a stupid thing to say," he said. "Rory's mattress was here when I went down to confession with the other seventh graders. They will tell you I was in the chapel until after my confession. And Larry Williams will tell you that I came out of the chapel the same time he did and went straight to the library. I wouldn't have any trouble convincing Father Rodriguez that I couldn't possibly have taken the mattress."

Tom's innocent act convinced Sweyn that The Great Brain knew where the mattress was. He decided to appeal to Tom's money-loving heart. "Let us assume you didn't take the mattress," he said. "What is your price for putting your great brain to work to solve the mystery?"

Tom considered for a moment. "I just might do it if

all you eighth graders raise your right hands and swear never to do anything that will make any seventh grader get any demerits."

"What are you talking about?" Sweyn asked.

"Who do you think mussed up my bunk twice and got me ten demerits?" Tom asked. "And who do you think took my textbook and planted it in the library to get me another five demerits? Nobody but Rory Flynn."

Sweyn turned to face Rory. "That was a dirty low-down trick to pull," he said. "And if I'd caught you at it you would be missing more than a mattress. You would be missing a couple of teeth."

"Listen to who is talking," Tom said, really enjoying himself. "The same brother who doesn't want me to get into a fight."

Rory looked as guilty as a fox caught in a chicken coop. "I was just playing a joke on him," he said to Sweyn.

"Making a fellow get demerits is no joke," Sweyn said.

Tom touched Sweyn on the arm. "If I'd really put my great brain to work on it," he said, "and was willing to do such a low-down thing, I could have got Rory expelled in one week."

"I won't do it again," Rory promised.

"You can bet you won't," Sweyn said, "because you and all of us eighth graders are now going to take an oath that we will never do anything that might get a seventh grader demerits."

Tom couldn't help chuckling to himself as he heard all the eighth graders take the oath.

"All right, T.D.," Sweyn said. "Where is Rory's mattress?"

"How should I know?" Tom asked. "I only promised to put my great brain to work on the mystery. But don't worry. I'm sure I'll solve it before Father Rodriguez's inspection tomorrow morning."

Rory pointed at his bunk. "You mean I've got to sleep on those hard boards tonight?" he asked.

Tom shrugged. "I sure as heck don't know where else you can sleep," he said. "These bunks aren't big enough for two fellows."

That was one night when everybody in the dormitory had something to say after lights-out. Tom started it.

"Boy, oh, boy," he said. "This mattress sure feels nice and soft."

"Mine too," Jerry said.

"I'm sure glad I'm not sleeping on boards," Phil said.

Larry Williams patted his pillow. "A fellow never really appreciates a good mattress until he has to sleep without one," he said.

And poor old Rory had to lie there on hard wooden slats listening.

Tom remained awake until he was sure all the other kids were asleep. Then he awakened Jerry. They got the mattress from the storeroom and placed it on the floor beside Rory's bunk. Both of them fell asleep chuckling to themselves.

When the six o'clock bell rang in the morning, Rory got up, rubbing his sore muscles. When he saw the mattress he almost jumped out of his nightgown.

"Look at that!" he shouted. "My mattress is lying right there while I've been getting black and blue sleeping on those boards."

Then Rory walked over to Tom's bunk. "I'm not going to fight you," he said, "and I'm not going to mess with your great brain anymore. You leave me alone and I'll leave you alone."

Tom yawned and stretched. "That sounds fair enough," he said.

Tom didn't get any more demerits right up to the time he and Sweyn came home for the Christmas vacation. I was sure glad to see my brothers but couldn't help feeling a little jealous of Tom. Our foster brother Frankie had thought I was just about the greatest fellow in the world until he met Tom. Now he followed The Great Brain around adoringly like a little puppy.

Papa got Tom alone in the parlor the first thing. He gave him a good dressing down for that first month's bad report and the fifteen demerits he received in November. And having got that out of his system Papa said we could all enjoy the holidays.

I knew I would enjoy them because Papa told Tom to help me with the chores. I could tell from the look on Tom's face that he didn't like the idea of having to do chores on his vacation. That first night Mamma allowed Frankie and me to stay up until nine o'clock. Then we went up to the room we shared with Tom. The Great Brain sat on a chair and pulled off a shoe.

"What's new in town?" he asked.

"Nothing," I answered.

"You must be mistaken," he said. "There must be something new in town since I've been away."

"I'm not mistaken," I said. "I've been right here in Adenville all the time and it's just the same as it was when you left for the academy."

"I'll bet I can prove there is something new in town," he said. "If I can't, I'll do your share of the chores while I'm home. If I can, you do my share. Is it a bet?"

This was one bet I knew I was going to win. "It's a bet," I said.

Tom pointed at Frankie. "We didn't have an adopted brother when I left for the academy," he said. "And that makes Frankie something new in town."

I felt as stupid as a donkey trying to fly. Tom had been home less than one day and he had already connived me into doing his share of the chores.

Frankie came over to my bed. "I'll help, John," he said.

"The only one who can help me," I said sadly, "is the fellow who invents a muzzle for human beings like they have for dogs to keep my big mouth shut."

That made Tom and Frankie laugh but I didn't think it was funny.

The next morning I started the chores by filling up the woodbox in the kitchen. Mamma and Aunt Bertha were washing the breakfast dishes. Mamma kept looking at me with a funny expression. But she didn't say anything until I brought in the first bucketful of coal.

"Why isn't Tom D. helping you?" she asked.

I sure as heck didn't want my own mother to know she had given birth to a son so stupid he had bet there was nothing new in town.

"Tom and I made a deal," I said.

"What kind of a deal?" she asked.

"What's the difference?" I asked.

142

"The difference is that I asked you what kind of a deal," Mamma said. "Now you tell me."

"You'll be sorry if I do," I tried to warn her.

"Then let me be sorry," she said.

"Mamma," I said looking her right in the eye, "you gave birth to a son who is a stupid jackass."

I thought that would make her cry. Instead she sort of smiled.

"Let me be the judge of that," she said.

I told her about the bet I'd made with Tom.

"You tell Tom Dennis that I want to see him at once," she said when I finished.

I knew she was angry when she called Tom by his full name. I went into the backyard where Tom was pushing Frankie on the swing. I told him Mamma wanted to see him. I followed him and Frankie into the kitchen.

"Tom Dennis," Mamma said firmly, "give me a definition of a town."

"Why are you angry at me?" Tom asked. "And why do you want me to define a town?"

"Just do as I told you," Mamma said.

"A town," Tom said, "is a place where there are homes and places of business and people living that doesn't have a large enough population to be called a city."

"An excellent definition," Mamma said. "But you lose the bet you made with John D. and I will tell you why. Frankie came to Adenville many times with his parents and brother before they were killed in the land slide. Mr. Harmon at the Z.C.M.I. store knew him and so did a lot of other people his father did business with. So Frankie isn't anything new in town and you lose the bet."

I wasn't about to pass up a chance to rub salt in Tom's wounds after the way he had tried to flimflam me. I followed him down to the wood-and-coal shed.

"In case you've forgotten," I said, "after you fill all the woodboxes and coal buckets, you feed and water our team and our milk cow and Sweyn's mustang, Dusty, and the chickens."

I followed Tom around pouring salt into his wounds until he finished the chores. Then he said he had some important business and left. He came home for lunch with Sweyn and Papa.

"And now," Papa said as we all sat down to lunch, "please tell me, T.D., what you were doing reading all those back issues of the *Advocate*."

"I didn't tell you this morning," Tom said, "because I wanted you as a witness in front of Mamma." Then he told Papa about the bet we had made and how Mamma had ruled in my favor.

"It seems to me," Papa said when Tom finished, "that your mother is right."

"No she isn't," Tom said. "According to your own newspaper six new babies have been born in Adenville since I left for the academy. And six new babies are certainly something new in town. And that means J.D. lost the bet."

Papa shook his head as he looked across the table at me. "I'm afraid T.D. is right," he said. "And I hope this will teach you never to bet against The Great Brain again."

In spite of my having to do all the chores it turned out to be a happy Christmas. It didn't start out as one, though. I had an old worn catcher's mitt. I had told Papa I wanted a new mitt for Christmas and had showed him the Spalding's Decker Patent Boys' League catcher's mitt I wanted in the Sears Roebuck catalogue. I had let him know in plenty of time to order it.

I don't believe there was a more disappointed kid in the United States on Christmas morning than me. And I blamed it all on the fact that Papa couldn't resist every new invention he saw advertised. Our attic was full of crazy inventions which didn't work, like the butter churner you peddled instead of pumping by hand.

"I thought it would lighten your work, Tena," he had said to Mamma after discovering it wasn't worth a darn. And having passed the buck to Mamma that gave Papa the right to order the next new invention he saw advertised. But I didn't dream he would order some crazy invention for my Christmas present instead of the catcher's mitt.

On Christmas morning Tom, Frankie, and I put on our robes and ran down to the parlor with Sweyn right behind us. Presents were all around the Christmas tree and the red stockings on the mantelpiece were filled with candy. Sweyn received a beaut of a fly-fishing rod and reel with a box of fly hooks. Tom received a watch with a fob. Frankie received several toys. And what did I get? None of us knew. My present was a large leather-covered ball and a metal hoop with a net on it attached to some boards about three feet square. Papa had bought another of his crazy inventions for my Christmas present. Even Tom with his great brain didn't know what it was. Papa heard us talking and came into the room with a robe over his nightgown.

"Well, J.D.," he said as proud as if he had given me a catcher's mitt, "what do you think of it?"

145

"How can I think anything when I don't even know what it is?" I said, letting him know I was disappointed.

"It is the latest game that is going over big back East," Papa said. "I read about it some time ago but didn't come across it in a sporting-goods catalogue until recently."

"How do you play it?" Tom asked.

"I will show you after breakfast," Papa said.

During breakfast Papa told us the game was called basketball. It was originated by a man named Naismith in 1891. Since then it had been introduced as a competitive sport in several colleges and high schools back East. The board with the hoop and net on it was called the backboard.

After breakfast Papa got a hammer and some nails. Tom and Sweyn carried the backboard down to our shed. Papa nailed it to the alley side of the shed about six feet from the ground. All the time I was wishing we didn't have such mild winters in Adenville. Maybe if we had snow Papa would have bought me a sled instead.

Papa laid the hammer to one side. "I realized that we didn't have room for a regular basketball court," he said. "That is why I only bought one backboard instead of two. But you and your friends, J.D., can have a lot of fun playing with just one backboard. You can improvise a game. Draw a line in the dirt—what we will call the foul line— about twelve feet from the backboard. You and I will play T.D. and S.D. I'll start the game with a free throw."

Papa took the ball and toed the line I drew in the dirt. "The idea is to pass the ball through the hoop," Papa said. "The team who makes the most baskets wins the game."

It only took me a few minutes to realize that basketball, even with only one backboard, was a very exciting game. I forgave Papa for not getting me the catcher's mitt. Basketball was going to make me the most popular kid in Adenville. I was already mentally selecting teams from among my playmates.

Tom was very much interested in the game, but for a different reason. He put his arm around my shoulders after we finished playing.

"You can make a fortune," he said, "by charging kids to play basketball."

"I don't have a money-loving heart like you," I said. "Any friend of mine can play free any time he wants."

"Have it your way," Tom said. "But you won't need the rule book with only one backboard. And I'll get that sporting-goods catalogue from Papa."

"What are you going to do with them?" I asked.

"This is one game we can play at the academy," Tom said. "There isn't room enough for baseball or football or even for tennis. But we have a big gymnasium where we can play basketball."

"I thought all sports were forbidden," I said.

"I'm putting my great brain to work to change that," he said.

Christmas vacation came to an end. Papa's last words to Tom were that he expected The Great Brain to complete the rest of the school year without any demerits. For my money that was like expecting a kid not to eat any more candy.

CHAPTER TEN

Basketball and the Bishop

FATHER O'MALLEY MET Tom and Sweyn at the depot in Salt Lake City.

"You have a wonderful surprise waiting for you at the academy," he said to Tom after greeting them.

Tom was as curious as a scout bumblebee in the early spring. But the priest refused to tell him what the surprise was.

Father Rodriguez was sitting at his desk when Tom and Sweyn entered the office. And, wonder of wonders, the superintendent was actually smiling as he greeted them. Then he removed a letter from a drawer in the desk, handling it as if it were a precious document.

148

"This letter arrived for you two days ago," he said to Tom. "It is from the Vatican."

Tom had figured it would take about a month for his letter to reach the Pope and about a month for an answer. But after three months had passed with no answer he hadn't expected any.

"And all this time," Tom said, "I've been thinking Pope Leo wasn't going to bother to answer my letter."

Father Rodriguez pressed the letter against his chest. "Dear God in heaven," he said, "a letter from the Holy Father. What a priceless treasure. It is probably the only letter ever received in Utah from a Pope. You must let us put it in a glass case in the visitor's room for all to see."

Tom wasn't going to put the letter on display or even let the superintendent read it if it said what he thought it would. "You can exhibit the envelope with the Vatican postmark," he said. "But I don't know about the letter until I read it."

"Of course," Father Rodriguez said. "You can go into the library and read it right now."

Tom went into the library and opened the envelope. He was sure regretting he had ever written the Pope about Father Rodriguez and the academy. What if on the basis of his letter the Pope and Jesuit general had decided to get rid of Father Rodriguez? Tom's hands were trembling as he unfolded the letter. He breathed a sigh of relief when he discovered it was just a printed form which read:

Your communication to His Holiness Pope Leo XIII has been received at the Vatican. It is impossible for the Holy Father to personally answer the hundreds of letters he receives each month. In

149

the event your communication seeks spiritual guidance or advice on personal problems please consult your parish priest or the bishop of your diocese.

Tom folded the printed form and put it in his pocket. He knew if Sweyn and the other fellows knew he'd written to the Pope and just got back a printed form they would give him the good old raspberry. He certainly wasn't going to let anybody but his three friends know. And that gave him an idea. Why not let Father Rodriguez think he had actually received a letter from the Pope? It just might help him get a sports program going at the academy. He returned to the superintendent's office and handed just the envelope to Father Rodriguez.

"I'm sorry, Father," he said, "but what was inside the envelope is confidential." That was no lie, he told himself. He certainly wanted to keep it confidential that all he had received was a printed form.

"I understand, Thomas," the priest said. "But can you tell me what you wrote to His Holiness about?"

"It was about the academy," Tom answered. "Please Father, may I talk to you about it later?"

"Of course," the superintendent said. "You are both excused."

Sweyn was speechless until they left the office. "Do you mean to tell me that you wrote a letter to the Pope and he answered it?" he said. "I don't believe it. Let me see the letter."

"You heard me tell Father Rodriguez it was confidential," Tom said. "And what do I care what you believe or don't believe? I've got the letter right here in my pocket and nobody is ever going to see it."

After Tom had greeted his three friends and unpacked his suitcase he told them about the printed form.

"But Father Rodriguez thinks I got a letter from the Pope," he said, "and that is going to help us get some changes made around here."

"Like what?" Jerry asked.

Tom showed them the rule book on basketball and the sporting-goods catalogue. "The gymnasium has a hardwood floor and a high ceiling," he said. "It is ideal for a basketball court."

Jerry was doubtful. "I can tell you right now what Father Rodriguez is going to say," he said. "He will say we were sent here to get an education and not to play games."

"Not if I can convince him without lying that Pope Leo is in favor of a sports program," Tom said. "Meanwhile, I don't see any kids eating candy, which means that we had better get the candy store open as soon as possible. I'll make a trip to the grocery store Friday evening."

His three friends stared at him. Jerry was the first to speak.

"Mean to tell me you didn't bring any with you?" he asked.

"Why should I take that chance," Tom said, "when we've got our candy store?"

The class in calisthenics was the last class of the day for the seventh and eighth graders. Father Rodriguez always led the exercises dressed in a sweat shirt and gym pants. Tom waited until the class was over on Friday. He walked up to the superintendent, who was wiping sweat from his face with a towel.

"It is too bad the fellows don't have anything to do between now and suppertime," he said. "Do you believe in the old saying that a healthy body makes for a healthy mind?"

"Yes, Thomas," the priest answered. "That is why we have this class in calisthenics, to keep you boys physically fit."

"But that is only for one hour on school days," Tom said. "A growing boy needs a lot more exercise than that."

Father Rodriguez finished wiping the sweat from his face and stared at Tom. "What are you trying to tell me?" he asked.

"I think Pope Leo would like it if we had some sports here at the academy," Tom said. "Take this gymnasium. It could be fixed up so we could play basketball. And all the boys would get to play because there are five players on each team: a center, two guards, and two forwards. We could have a first and second team for each grade. And the seventh-grade teams could play against the eighth-grade teams."

"I have never heard of the game," Father Rodriguez said.

"A lot of schools back East play basketball now," Tom said. "And if we had basketball here we would be the first Catholic academy to introduce the sport."

Father Rodriguez shook his head. "Even if we could get permission from Pope Leo and the general of the Society of Jesus," he said, "we have no money in our budget for any athletic program."

"If each boy got just one dollar from his parents," Tom said, "we would have enough money to buy two backboards, a basketball, a referee's whistle, and enough paint for the foul lines and boundary lines. My mother always said the devil will find work for idle hands. Basketball would help to keep the fellows out of trouble."

"All right, Thomas," the superintendent said. "I can't see any possible harm in it in view of the fact that His Holiness apparently gave his blessing to an athletic program, and he must have consulted the Jesuit general about it."

Tom didn't say anything. Even with his great brain he couldn't think of anything to say without letting Father Rodriguez know he was jumping to the wrong conclusion.

Six weeks later the first basketball practice was held in the gymnasium with Father Rodriguez acting as coach. Practice continued for one week and then the superintendent picked the first and second teams for both grades. Sweyn and Rory made the eighth-grade first team with Rory as captain. Tom and Jerry made the seventh-grade first team with Tom as captain. Tom challenged the eighth-grade first team to a game. He and his teammates soon discovered they played under a disadvantage because the eighth graders were all taller than they were. Tom put his great brain to work on how to beat them. But his team kept on losing to the eighth-grade first team, although they could beat the eighth-grade second team.

Basketball made Tom such a hero to all the fellows that Sweyn wrote to Papa and Mamma about it. Papa considered the introduction of basketball in a western school newsworthy enough to put on the wire services to the Salt Lake City newspapers. Sports writers from both newspapers came to the academy to watch a game between the seventh- and eighth-grade first teams. The stories they printed attracted the attention of superintendents of other parochial and public schools, and they requested permission to come and watch. There were so many requests that Father Rodriguez decided to invite them all to a game on a Friday afternoon.

Tom held a secret practice with the seventh grade first and second teams to prepare for the big game.

"My great brain has figured out a way we might beat the eighth graders this time," he said as his teammates crowded around him in the gymnasium. "Instead of leaving one guard at our end of the court, all five of us will take the ball down to the other end. That will give us man for man instead of just four of us against their five players. And with our superior speed we should be able to get a lot of baskets that way."

Jerry shook his head. "I don't think it's wise to leave our basket unguarded," he said.

"Let's try it right now," Tom said. "The second team will use the system against us and see if they do any better than last time."

The second team piled up more points in less time than they ever had before and Tom was confident his system would work. But his money-loving heart told him not to bet any money unless he had a sure thing. And that made his great brain come up with a plan.

That evening after supper he gathered the eighth graders around him in the dormitory. He opened a notebook.

"I have here the final scores of all the games played by our first team against your first team," he said. "And if I add them all up you have beaten us by an average of eighteen points each game."

Rory grinned. "And we'll beat you by more than that Friday," he said.

Rory didn't know it but he had walked right into a trap.

"I don't believe you can beat us by eighteen points Friday," Tom said.

"Wouldn't care to bet on it, would you?" Rory asked.

"Let me get this straight," Tom said. "If you beat us by eighteen or more points you win the bet. If you beat us by less than eighteen points I win the bet. Is that right?"

Rory and all the other eighth graders nodded their heads.

Before setting up the eighth graders for the bet Tom had got his bag of money from under the statue of Saint Francis and placed it under his pillow. He went to his bunk and took it out.

"Step right up and make your bets," he said, jingling the coins in the bag. "I'm covering all of them."

Those eighth graders were sure confident their team would win by eighteen or more points! Every one of them put down a bet. Tom stood to win or lose almost five dollars.

But on Friday morning it didn't look as if that game would ever be played. Father Rodriguez interrupted a history lesson to call Tom from the classroom. At first Tom thought he had found out about the betting on the game. But he knew he was wrong when he entered the superintendent's office. He had never seen a Catholic bishop in his life but he knew he was looking at one now. The heavyset man with iron-gray hair sitting at the desk was wearing the purple robe and the ring of a bishop.

The Right Reverend Francis Miglaccio was the bishop of the diocese that at the time consisted of four states. He only came to Salt Lake City once a year. What brought about this unusual visit was a clipping from one of the Salt Lake City newspapers about basketball being played at the Catholic Academy for Boys. Some Catholic who was against a sports program in a Catholic school had mailed it to him.

"I am your bishop," the man said in a commanding voice, picking up the envelope that had been received from the Vatican. "And you, I presume, are the Thomas D. Fitzgerald, Esquire to whom this envelope is addressed. Father Rodriguez has informed me that you obtained permission from His Holiness Pope Leo XIII to introduce an athletic program in this school. I find this difficult to believe. So you will show me the letter you say you received from the Holy Father."

Tom knew he was caught. There was no hope for escape. He couldn't lie to a bishop or refuse an order given by a bishop. Not even his great brain could get him out of this one.

"I didn't receive a letter from the Pope," he confessed. "It was just a printed form sent to thousands of Catholics who write to him."

Father Rodriguez turned pale and pressed his hand to his forehead. "But you told me you had received a letter from Pope Leo," he protested. "And you also told me that he had given his permission for us to introduce an athletic program here."

"I confess that I led you to believe I'd received a letter from the Pope," Tom said. "But I never actually said I had received a letter. And I admit I said I thought Pope Leo would approve of us having basketball here. But what I think and what the Holy Father may think are two different things."

Father Rodriguez clasped his hands as if in prayer. "You tricked me," he said sadly. "I know you have always disliked me, Thomas, but I never thought you could do such a thing to me."

"I admit I didn't like you at first," Tom said. "But I like you fine now, just fine. And I also honor and respect you."

"Bless you for that," Father Rodriguez said.

Tom turned his head to look at the bishop. "There hasn't been one student who has received any demerits since basketball started," he said. "The game is being played in many schools back East. And this afternoon superintendents of parochial and public schools in Salt Lake City are coming to watch the game. I am sorry for getting Father Rodriguez into trouble with you but I can't see where any harm has been done."

Bishop Miglaccio leaned forward. "There will be no basketball game this afternoon," he said. "There never has been and never will be an athletic program in a Catholic school. You are dismissed."

Tom walked over and knelt before Father Rodriguez. "Forgive me, Father," he cried, "I didn't mean to hurt you or to get you into any trouble. I just wanted to make the academy a place where fellows would want to go to school and not just have to go because their parents sent them. I wanted the fellows to be proud of the academy and have some school spirit and some fun once in a while. I'm sorry, Father. As God is my judge I am truly sorry. Please forgive me."

Father Rodriguez made the sign of the cross. "I forgive you, Thomas," he said.

Tom stood up. "Thank you, Father," he said.

Tom didn't bother going back to the classroom. He knew he was going to be expelled. He went up to the dormitory instead. He got his suitcase from under his bunk and began packing. When he finished he got his bag of money from under the statue of Saint Francis and put it in the suitcase. He would wait until noon to return the money bet on the game and say good-bye to Sweyn and his friends. He was sitting on his bunk with his back toward the doorway, so he wasn't aware Father Rodriguez had entered the dormitory until the priest spoke.

"What are you doing, Thomas?" the superintendent asked.

"I know I'm going to be expelled," Tom said. "I'll leave as soon as I say good-bye to my brother and my friends. I have some money and will take the next train home."

"Unpack your things," Father Rodriguez said. "You aren't going to be expelled. Bishop Miglaccio has decided to reserve judgment until after the basketball game this afternoon."

Tom couldn't have been more surprised if he'd been told that Bishop Miglaccio was going to be the referee for the game.

"What . . . what made him change his mind?" he asked.

"He told me it was what you said to me," the superintendent said. "And bless you for that, Tom."

If Tom was surprised before, he was now doubly surprised. "You called me Tom," he said.

"You once told me you preferred it to Thomas," Father Rodriguez said smiling. "And now you had better be getting back to your classroom."

When the first teams of the seventh and eighth grades took to the floor of the gymnasium that afternoon it was packed with spectators. After a few warm-ups the game began with Father Rodriguez as referee and Father O'Malley using a large blackboard, chalk, and eraser to keep score.

Tom's plan of using a five-man offense worked quite well. His team was behind only six points at the end of the first half. But during the second half the eighth-grade team began using the system also. Going into the fourth quarter the score was twenty-eight to fourteen. With five minutes left to play Tom called for a time-out. The score was now thirty-two to sixteen.

"When we get the ball," Tom said in the huddle, "don't try to make any baskets. Just keep passing it around at our end of the court."

Jerry got the ball and instead of taking it down toward the eighth-grade basket he dribbled it toward his own backboard. The eighth-grade team waited at their end of the court. They waited and waited and then it finally dawned on them that they were only winning by sixteen points. Down the court they came. But Tom's team

had a lot more speed and just kept passing the ball to one another until the whistle blew ending the game. Tom's great brain had made him four dollars and eighty cents because his team was beat by only sixteen points.

Bishop Miglaccio held mass in the academy chapel on Sunday. Afterward he called Tom to the superintendent's office.

"I enjoyed the basketball game," he said. "And I was pleased with the congratulations Father Rodriguez and I received from the superintendents of other schools. A league is going to be formed next year. Do you know what that means, Thomas?"

"It means you have made a lot of kids happy," Tom said.

"That isn't quite what I meant," Bishop Miglaccio said. "It means there will be interscholastic rivalry in basketball next year. Your eighth-grade academy team will be playing the eighth-grade teams of other schools. I shall be here for the final game of the season and expect to see the academy win the championship."

"We will win it," Tom said confidently. "I'll have all summer to put my great brain to work on plays."

"Oh, yes," Bishop Miglaccio said. "Father Rodriguez has told me about your great brain. Have you ever thought of repaying God for giving it to you by becoming a priest?"

"I haven't decided what I want to be yet," Tom said.

"Now before I leave," Bishop Miglaccio said. "I want you to tell us what you put in that letter you wrote to Pope Leo."

"What I put in the letter doesn't count anymore," Tom said.

"We would still like to know," Bishop Miglaccio said.

Tom was so ashamed that he couldn't even look at Father Rodriguez. "For one thing," he said, "I wrote that this academy was more like a reform school than an academy. I know now I was wrong about that. If Father Rodriguez didn't maintain discipline the kids would walk all over him and the other priests. And I wrote that I thought the punishments were too severe. I was wrong about that too. I know now that making a boy get up at four o'clock in the morning to peel potatoes for breaking a rule is going to make him think twice before he does it again. But the worst thing of all was that I asked the Pope to replace Father Rodriguez."

Tom raised his head and looked at the bishop. "I was dead wrong about that too," he said. "My trouble and the trouble with all the fellows was that we were afraid of Father Rodriguez. We feared him because he could hand down demerits and punishments and even expel us. And no one can like anybody he is afraid of. That is why we disliked him. But my great brain is going to change all that."

Bishop Miglaccio stared at Tom. "And just how do you propose to overcome this fear the boys have of Father Rodriguez?" he asked.

"The same way I did it myself," Tom answered. "I am going to convince them that they don't really fear Father Rodriguez but themselves. They are really afraid they might break a rule or do something that will get them demerits or punishment. And if they are going to dislike anybody because of this fear, they should start disliking themselves. When I get through I'll personally guarantee there won't be one fellow in this academy who can honestly say he dislikes Father Rodriguez."

Bishop Miglaccio shook his head slowly. "It will be a great loss to the Church if you don't become a priest," he said.

Father Rodriguez smiled. "I am glad you wrote that letter and told us what you wrote," he said.

"You are?" Tom asked with surprise. "Why, Father?"

"It is proof you have matured a great deal since writing it," the superintendent said, "and helping boys to mature is a very important part of my job here."

Well, all I can say is that maybe Tom did mature a great deal during his first year at the academy, but he sure as heck didn't reform. He didn't get any more demerits for the rest of the school year, which made Papa and Mamma happy. But I knew it was only because Tom got mature enough not to get caught. He ran his candy store full blast until the last week of school. And he was the only kid in the history of the Catholic Academy for Boys who made going to school a profitable financial venture. When he removed the paper bag from under the statue of Saint Francis on the last day of school there was over thirty dollars in it. On the train ride home Tom sat staring out the window for a long time. "I'll bet I know what you are thinking about," Sweyn said. "You are wondering what you are going to do with all that money you made at the academy."

"That's a bet you would lose," Tom said. "I was thinking that all the kids in Adenville must have saved up quite a bit of money since I've been away. And also about all the presents they received for Christmas and their birthdays. Now please be quiet. I've got to put my great brain to work on plans for making this a very profitable summer vacation."

What Tom should have said was that he was going to put his great brain and his money-loving heart to work on plans for swindling the kids in Adenville during the summer vacation. It had taken me a long time but my little brain had finally figured out what made Tom tick. A fellow with a great brain and a normal heart becomes a scientist or a philosopher. It wasn't Tom's great brain that made him a confidence man but his money-loving heart.

And to think my college-educated father had been foolish enough to hope the Jesuit priests at the academy would reform my brother. I had only a little brain and a fourth-grade education but I knew better. For my money, the Pope himself couldn't reform Tom unless he agreed to make The Great Brain a cardinal. And then just maybe Tom would reform. I say *just maybe* because if The Great Brain couldn't make a deal with the college of cardinals to make him the next pope, he would probably refuse to become a cardinal.

About the Author and Artist

JOHN D. FITZGERALD's stories of the Great Brain are based on his own childhood in Utah, where he had a conniving older brother named Tom. These reminiscences have led to three popular earlier books, *The Great Brain, More Adventures of the Great Brain,* and *Me and My Little Brain.* Mr. Fitzgerald is also the author of several adult books, including *Papa Married a Mormon.* He now lives with his wife in Titusville, Florida.

MERCER MAYER's delightfully droll illustrations appear in all of *The Great Brain* books. He is also the author-illustrator of many books of his own, including the three wordless *A Boy, a Dog and a Frog* books, *There's a Nightmare in My Closet,* and *A Special Trick.* Mr. Mayer was born in Little Rock, Arkansas, and now lives with his wife Marianna in Sea Cliff, New York.